Sheltering

Macy

Stone Knight's MC
Book 8

Megan Fall

Sheltering Macy
Published by Megan Fall

Dedication

To my readers

You guys rock! Thank you so much for your love
and support!

Contents

Chapter One
Preacher

Preacher walked into the common room and froze at the sight before him.

"Will you get your goddamned tongue out of my sister's mouth," he roared. "I'm in the fucking room."

Shadow smirked at him as he slowly pulled away from Tiffany. "Well, you weren't in the room when I stuck it in her mouth," he replied cheekily.

"Fuck me," Preacher grumbled. "Another god damned comedian." Then he turned on his heel and furiously stomped to his office.

Preacher shoved open the door, then promptly kicked it shut after he was in. He crossed the room and collapsed in his chair, placing his elbows on the desk. Then he leaned over to rest his head in his hands. His club used to be full of badass bikers, now it was full of pussy whipped men. He missed the old days, the days before pink rooms and women drama.

Preacher tried to contain the couples by placing the bikers and their women in cabins, but that meant the clubhouse was getting fucking emptier. He also tried to recruit, but it was hard to find good men worthy of The Stone Knight's patch.

He looked up when the door opened and Steele barged in. "Don't you fucking knock?" Preacher growled in annoyance.

Steele gave him a lazy grin. "Why the fuck would I knock? Seems all you ever do these days is sit behind that fucking desk and pout."

Preacher picked up a stapler and threw it at the brother, but Steele easily ducked out of the way as he chuckled.

"What the fucks your problem now? I heard you yelling from down the hall," Steele questioned.

"Fucking Shadow was making out with my sister again," Preacher sneered.

Steele laughed even harder. "They love each other brother. That's bound to happen. You just wait until you find a woman, then maybe you won't be so crusty."

"I'm not crusty," Preacher roared. He picked up a paper weight to throw at the brother next, but Steele wisely ducked back out the door. He moved quick too, probably getting that from hanging out with Trike. Now that little fucker could move.

Preacher stared at the closed door and leaned back in his chair. The bikers were dropping like flies, even Mario had a girl of his own now. He needed to start a pool on who would be next and make some fucking dough. At least get something out of it.

Preacher gave up on the paperwork he had planned to do and pushed out of his chair. When he walked back into the common room, he was happy to see Shadow and his sister were gone. He headed to the bar where Dragon and Navaho were sitting shooting the shit. Navaho instantly filled a glass with a shot of whiskey and passed it to him.

Drinking was what he needed to do now, he thought. Get rip-roaring drunk, then pass out in bed.

"You okay prez?" Dragon asked with a raised brow. Preacher was on his third shot and decided to be frank.

"I'm sick of the fucking girls roaming around all the time," he growled.

"Ah," Dragon snickered. "So you're jealous?"

"I'm not fucking jealous," Preacher instantly denied. He was ready to say more, but his cell chose that moment to go off. He pulled it from his back pocket and stared at Raid's name on the screen. They had placed the brother on the gate today, so that meant they had company.

"What?" Preacher greeted in agitation.

"Car pulled up to the gate. Man and woman inside. Apparently they're family of Snake's," Raid explained.

"Call the brother and have him meet me at the gate. I'm on my way," Preacher ordered.

"Right," Raid responded before hanging up.

Preacher turned to Dragon. "Snake has family at the gate. Care to join me?" he questioned his Sargent at Arms.

"Wouldn't miss it," Dragon grinned as he pushed out of his chair and followed Preacher out the door.

Halfway there they met Snake. "You got family?" Preacher asked the prospect.

"Pop and his daughter," Snake revealed tightly.

Preacher raised his eyebrows at the brothers wording. "Not your sister?" he questioned in surprise.

"No," Snake snapped angrily. "She's not my fucking sister."

Preacher shrugged as they reached the gate, knowing he'd figure out what was going on in a minute. He had no idea what to expect though. With this club, everything was a crap shoot.

Chapter Two
Preacher

Preacher nodded at Raid when he arrived, and the brother hit the button to open the gate. They stepped back as it rolled open and the car drove through. When he looked towards Snake, the brother was practically sneering at the car. Preacher hated crap like this. Drama drove him fucking nuts.

Once the car was through Raid closed the gate. Preacher headed straight for the driver's door with Steele and Dragon flanking him. "Can you get out of the car?" he ordered Snake's father.

The man nodded nervously and stepped out. When Preacher turned, expecting Snake to be there, he found the brother still standing where he'd left him.

"Snake," Preacher roared in annoyance. "Get your goddamned ass over here." The brother actually scowled more before dragging his feet in their direction. Steele started chuckling beside him, finding the whole thing funny. "Fucking daycare," Preacher growled.

When Snake was finally beside them, Preacher sighed and turned back to his father.

"What brings you to our door?" he questioned.

"Got myself into some trouble," the man told him.

"Fuck me," Snake barked, then he turned and started to head back towards the clubhouse, obviously finished with his father.

"You take one more step in that direction, I'm going to let Dragon teach you a goddamned lesson in manners," Preacher shouted in warning. Snake immediately halted and turned back to them.

"You bring trouble to my door?" Preacher growled at Snake's father, as he twisted back around.

"No I did not," his father answered.

"You're fucking gambling again," Snake accused as he joined them.

His father hung his head. "Got in a little too deep this time."

"What's your name?" Preacher growled.

"Wes," the man answered.

"Well Wes," Preacher acknowledged. "We don't pay off debts."

"Don't expect you too," he quickly interjected. "Not why I'm here."

"Then spit it out," Snake ordered as he crossed his arms and glared at his father.

Wes turned to the car and motioned, for who Preacher assumed was the sister, to get out. Then he watched as the door slowly opened and a girl got out.

She looked to be slightly taller than the other girls, but not by much. With Preacher's height, he'd still tower over her by at least a foot. She had the prettiest strawberry blond hair, and the tiniest waist he'd ever seen. He could do nothing but stare. She was the most stunning thing he had ever seen. Her eyes darted around the area nervously, and the action reminded him of a hummingbird.

Growling in annoyance and shaking himself out of his stupor, he turned back to Wes. "What the hell has this got to do with her?"

"The man I owe money to threatened her. He wants to take her as payment," Wes told them.

"So what's the problem?" Snake pushed, not looking at his sister once.

Preacher turned and moved so he was in the brothers face.

"You like prospecting for this club?" he sneered with barely controlled anger.

"I do," Snake growled in response.

"Family means everything," Preacher spat. "You don't disrespect your sister like that, you hear me."

"I fucking hear you," Snake returned while holding onto his anger.

"Watch your fucking mouth. You're treading on thin ground," Preacher growled. Then he turned his attention back to Wes.

"What do you want from us?" he asked.

"I want Snake to look after his sister while I figure out a way to pay off my debt," Wes explained.

Snake opened his mouth to say god knows what, but Preacher glared at him, and he instantly shut it.

"Snake's only a prospect," he told Wes. "We only take in family of patched members or their women," he felt the need to explain.

Wes turned to Snake then. "I can't keep her safe and I don't want him to get his hands on her. You're the only person I trust with her safety," he pleaded.

Dragon instantly turned to Snake. "You got somewhere you stayed in before you prospected?" he demanded furiously.

Snake dropped his head and then spoke to the ground. "I still have my apartment for another couple weeks," he admitted.

Preacher nodded. "You take her fucking there. Make sure she gets settled. Then we fucking talk," he ordered.

"What did she do to you anyway?" Steele asked, trying to get a read on the brothers attitude towards the girl.

"Killed my mother," Snake growled, shocking them all. Then he moved around the car, reached into the back, and pulled out a duffle bag.

Preacher's head whipped around to face the girl. A tear was rolling down her cheek as she looked at her brother, with devastation clearly written all over her face. When Snake ordered her to follow, she dutifully did as requested. Preacher caught her eye as she walked passed.

"How the fuck did you kill her?" he asked incredulously.

Another tear fell as she whispered five heartbreaking words. "She gave birth to me."

Preacher watched her walk away and once more thought of a hummingbird. Only this time the hummingbird was broken, and for some unknown reason, that fucking bothered him.

Chapter Three
Macy

Macy kept her head down the entire time she sat in the car. She was embarrassed and ashamed. Her father started gambling when her mother died, and every year it was growing considerably worse. He had good runs, but they never lasted long. This time owed a considerable amount of money, and he was terrified for her safety.

Macy tried not to look at any of the bikers, but her eyes drifted to her brother every so often. It absolutely killed her that he hated her so much. He helped raise her when their father was at work, but he never showed her an ounce of love.

When she was being delivered their mother suffered several complications. It came down to a choice of saving either her or Macy. Unfortunately, their mother had been coherent and had chosen Macy. Some days Macy wished she hadn't. Snake had been five at the time, and their mother had been his entire world. It destroyed him when she died. Of course, he blamed Macy for her death. He had wanted their mother to choose herself instead.

Their father had attempted repeatedly to change Snake's mind. Over the years he had begged and pleaded, then he tried to force the issue, finally he used guilt and told him that his mother would have been crushed over his attitude. Nothing worked, Snake simply held onto his hate let it fester.

Macy's attention was suddenly drawn to another biker. He was slightly taller than the others, and he stood in front. He had wavy, short, jet black hair, a moustache, a trimmed beard, and black tattoos covered both his arms. He was breathtaking. Snake had been infatuated with bikers since he was fifteen, and when he talked, she always paid attention. She understood right away that this man was the president.

He seemed furious by Snake's attitude, and it looked like he was quickly loosing his patience. Snake seemed to be holding his tongue though, so the biker turned back to her father. They talked for a minute, then her father motioned for her to get out.

Macy climbed out of the car with her head down and was just in time to catch Snake tell the men she had killed their mother. Some men gasped, and she couldn't hide the heartache she felt from Snake's words. She watched as her brother snatched her duffle bag from the car, and she knew that meant she should follow him.

As Macy passed the president, he caught her eye. She couldn't believe how intense his stare was. It was almost like he could see through her, and that unnerved her. She also felt a strong pull to him, and that terrified her.

"How did you kill her?" the man questioned gently. He didn't seem repulsed by her, or angered by what Snake said. He almost seemed curious.

"She gave birth to me," Macy whispered. Then she dropped her head, severing the contact, and kept walking.

Snake led her to an older looking truck. He threw her duffle in the bed and climbed in the drivers seat. Sighing, Macy opened the passenger door and climbed in as well. He started the truck without a word and pulled through the gate. She was surprised to see her father had already left. She hoped he would be okay, even though she knew her thoughts should be on herself.

Macy glanced at the president one last time and found his eyes still on her. The intense stare was back, and she couldn't look away. She even turned slightly in the seat so she could watch him longer. When Snake turned down the road, and she lost sight of him, she finally gave up.

"Thank you for helping me," Macy told her brother as she faced the front once more. "I know you didn't want to, and I appreciate it."

Snake looked at her a minute, then sighed and nodded. After driving for about ten minutes he stopped at a laundry mat. He turned off the truck, climbed out, and retrieved her duffle from the bed. Confused, she climbed out as well.

Macy followed him to the back of the building and up a rickety set of stairs. It was then she realized there was an apartment above the laundry mat. He unlocked the door, and she followed him in.

Inside was a small living room and kitchen, and she could see a bedroom down the hall. It was clean and tidy, but sparsely furnished and a bit run down.

"I've got this place paid up for the next two weeks. The laundry mat downstairs is run by the landlords. Tell them you're related to me and they'll give you a job. Grocery store is a block away," Snake explained.

Macy watched as he placed a set of keys on the counter. Then he dug into his pocket and pulled out a few twenties. He placed them on the counter as well.

"Spend it sparingly," Snake ordered. Then he turned and walked out.

Macy stared at the door, realizing he hadn't even bothered to leave his number.

Chapter Four
Preacher

Preacher sat at his desk and tried to concentrate on the numbers he was desperately trying to make balance. No matter how many times he entered them, the damn things wouldn't come out right. He pushed away from his desk and dragged his hands through his hair in frustration. Trike was now in charge of the books, but with Misty days away from giving birth, he'd told the nervous biker to stay with her. He regretted that decision more and more though.

As he leaned back and stared at the ceiling, a pretty face popped into his head. Every time he stopped to breathe these days that happened. Macy had shown up at the clubhouse three days ago, and she was all he could think about. He'd had plenty of women, and some he really liked, but none of them affected him the way she did. He had only seen her once, but it was enough to drive him bat shit crazy.

When Snake had gotten back from taking Macy wherever the hell he dropped her off, Preacher had dragged the prospect into his office and given him hell. If he wanted to remain prospecting for the Knight's, he better change his attitude, or get the fuck out.

When Preacher questioned him about why he hated his sister, Snake had stuck with his original answer. That had only pissed him off more. When Preacher explained a newborn had nothing to do with the decision that had been made, Snake had only shrugged.

Preacher's own mother had died of cancer when he was small, so he understood how devastating it was. But, that was no reason to blame Macy. Both of them grew up without a mother, and Preacher explained they should have had each other's back. When Snake only shrugged, Preacher had furiously walked away. He'd give the brother two weeks, and if his attitude didn't improve, or shit hit the fan, he was done with the fucker.

Preacher needed to learn more about the situation Snake's father Wes was in. It was now affecting club business, and even though Snake was only a prospect, he didn't need any more trouble coming to his door. Preacher didn't want to admit he was worried about the girl either, but when Wes had admitted the loan shark wanted her as payment, he had seen red.

He picked up his cell and hit Mario's button. The man answered on the first ring. Getting Mario to become part of the club had been a fucking great idea. Mario still ran his lucrative business, but he now lived on club land with his girl, and was more accessible than before.

"Preacher," Mario greeted. "What's up? Need some new ideas about how to lock Dagger in his room," he chuckled.

"You got a minute," Preacher questioned with a hint of a growl, completely ignoring the joke.

Mario caught the growl and read the vibe, and Preacher appreciated the serious tone Mario instantly switched too.

"What do you need?" Mario questioned.

"Snake's father showed at the gate with his daughter Macy a couple days ago," Preacher told him.

Mario sighed. "Yeah, I heard about that. Heard Snake was an ass too."

Preacher wasn't surprised that word had traveled fast through his club. "Apparently his dad is heavily into gambling and has gotten himself in over his head. He owes a loan shark some dough, but I don't know who the fucker is, and I don't know how much he's in for."

"What's the name of Snake's dad?" Mario inquired.

Preacher told him everything he knew, which wasn't fucking much. "You need to find this asshole, because if this debt isn't paid, he wants the daughter instead."

He could hear Mario's cursing through the phone. All of them condoned violence against women. "I'll get Trent and Nick on it right away." Then he paused a minute. "Snake's only a prospect, he's not an official part of the club yet, why get involved?"

"I'm not getting involved, but I don't need fuckers trying to blow up my compound again either. The more I know the better," Preacher declared.

Mario chuckled. "Right. Dagger will get a hard on if he thinks dynamite may be needed again."

"Fucker stock piles the shit," Preacher agreed with a frown. "What's my timeline?" he pushed.

"I should have something by morning," Mario promised.

"Appreciated," Preacher sighed, then promptly hung up.

As he leaned back, he thought of the girl once more. Things were getting fucking complicated.

Chapter Five
Macy

Macy stared at the little Chinese woman in stunned silence. She had come in to explain that she was Snake's sister, and would be taking over the apartment. She had also mentioned Snake told her she may be able to get a job at the laundromat. The Chinese lady had responded, but it wasn't sinking in.

Because Macy hadn't answered, the Chinese lady looked extremely irritated. "You work five days a week. Hours are seven until three," she repeated. But that wasn't the part that Macy was having trouble with. "You work in steam room. Feed clothes in hot rollers."

Macy looked around the steam room they were currently standing in with trepidation. The hot rollers were massive and took up half a wall, but it was the smoke rising from them that terrified her. One wrong move, and she'd find herself badly burned.

She turned back to the lady and pleaded with her. "Can't I just fold the laundry?" she questioned nervously.

The Chinese lady threw her hands up in the air and Macy took a small step back. "You steam clothes, then fold clothes," she angrily demanded. "You want job or not?"

Macy sighed in defeat. She'd already been to the few other businesses in town, and no one else would hire her. She would have called her brother, but she knew he'd only yell at her for not coming here in the first place, like he had told her to.

"Fine," Macy warily agreed. "When can I start?"

"You come in tomorrow morning, seven o'clock," her new boss demanded. "I pay you cash each week. You be on time."

Macy nodded, thanked the lady, then quickly fled. She knew the job would be hard, but she needed money to pay the rent. She climbed up the rickety stairs, holding the rail the whole way, and unlocked the door to the apartment. Macy hated living here, it was small, and it was dark. She collapsed on the couch and pulled the money she had left from her pocket.

Macy had thirty dollars, from the original sixty Snake had left her. The cupboards had been bare, and Macy had been forced to spend some money on groceries. Of course she was used to being on a budget, thanks to her fathers gambling. She bought a lot of ramen noodles, a couple apples, a loaf of bread, a jar of peanut butter, and a carton of orange juice. Macy figured she could water down the juice to make it last longer. She also bought toilet paper, a bottle of glass cleaner, laundry detergent and some basic bathroom supplies.

Macy spent the rest of the day washing the bedding in the bathtub, along with the tiny amount of clothes she had with her. She had then used her hairdryer to dry them as best she could. She absolutely refused to go downstairs to do her laundry. She had a feeling the Chinese lady would yell at her and charge her.

Macy moved to the cupboard and grabbed one of the packets of noodles. Then she filled a pot with water and placed it on the stove to boil. Ten minutes later she was sitting on the couch, staring at the wall as she ate. She was used to being alone, but she really wished she had company. Sometimes the quiet got to be too much.

When Macy was done, she leaned back and stared up at the ceiling. As she had done for the last couple nights, she thought of the huge biker. He had taken her breath away with his good locks and growly voice, and he was always on her mind. She knew she'd probably never see him again, but she couldn't help wondering what would happen if she did.

Macy closed her eyes and dreamed of him sweeping her off her feet. They'd laugh, they'd kiss, he'd hold her tight, and everything would be perfect. He'd love her more than life and treat her like a priceless treasure.

Macy shook her head, knowing it was only a ridiculous pipe dream, and headed back to the kitchen to dump her container. After a quick glass of water she headed to bed. She undressed and slipped on the tee she had long ago stolen from her brother. She used to do his laundry, and he never noticed it was missing. As she fell asleep, she held tight to her fantasy and dreamed of the huge biker once more.

Chapter Six
Macy

Macy dragged herself carefully up the rickety stairs to her apartment and unlocked the door. She made it as far as the couch, before falling onto it. She had suffered through her first day of work, and she absolutely hated it.

That little Chinese lady, who she had found out was named Mrs. Tang, was a slave driver. Macy had gone slowly, as she was completely terrified of the hot steamers, and Mrs. Tang threatened to dock her pay if she didn't go faster. They glared at each other, until Macy finally relented and tried to speed up.

She was sweaty, she was exhausted, and she was starving. She had hurried upstairs on her break and eaten a container of noodles, but she worked that off hours ago. Macy closed her eyes, figuring she'd just rest for a minute, and then fell promptly to sleep.

When she eventually woke, it surprised Macy to see it was dark outside. She sat up groggily and rubbed the sleep from her eyes. When her stomach growled, she remembered it had been a long time since she last ate. Sighing, she climbed to her feet, headed to the tiny kitchen, and made herself a peanut butter sandwich. She washed it down with a glass of water.

Then still feeling the sweat that coated her skin, Macy knew she better have a shower. The last thing she wanted was to deal with dirty sheets. She grabbed some clothes and locked herself in the bathroom. Leaning down, she turned on the water, then stripped as she waited for it to heat up. Thankfully it only took a minute, and she was grateful. She grabbed the lever and pulled, so the water came out the shower head, then climbed inside.

Macy didn't even get the chance to wash her hair, when the shower head cracked and fell, hitting her on the forehead. She cried out from both the pain, and from the jet of water that blasted her in the same spot the shower head had hit. She sputtered and tried to move, but the force of the water was too strong, and it slammed her against the back wall.

Desperate, she lifted her foot and kicked the stupid lever so the water went back to coming out the tap.

Macy fought to hold back the tears as she turned around, turned off the water, and climbed out to survey the damage to her head. The shower head had hit her just below her hairline, and of course it as bleeding. She quickly cleaned off the blood, bandaged it, and then got dressed.

Macy didn't know much about shower heads, but when she examined it, it looked like the nozzle had literally snapped and then fallen off. She was curious about how long it had been on there, because when she got a good look at it, it looked ancient.

Sighing, she fisted it in her hand and headed down to the laundry mat. She wasn't in the mood to fight with Mrs. Tang, but of course that's what ended up happening. She showed her landlord and new boss the shower head and asked her as nicely as she could to fix it. Mrs. Tang took one look at it and declared it was her fault, refusing to help. The stupid lady then turned and stomped away.

Macy would have called Snake, but she didn't have his number, and she didn't have a way to get there. The compound was about fifteen minutes away by car, by foot it would take her hours, and it was dark. She headed back up to her apartment and looked around in defeat. Knowing she had no other choice, she grabbed her measly thirty dollars, threw the damn shower head in a grocery bag, and headed out. The hardware store was about a ten-minute walk away.

Macy trudged down the quiet street and was almost there when she heard the distinctive sound of a motorcycle coming up behind her. She knew her chances of it being Snake were slim, but when she heard it stop directly behind her, she figured it had to be him.

Huffing in agitation, she slowly turned around. Then she gasped as she found herself staring into the eyes of the beautiful biker she was always dreaming about.

"Where you headed Hummingbird?" the biker growled as he eyed her curiously.

Macy blinked at him as she watched him climb off his Harley and head towards her. Then what he said slowly registered.

"Hummingbird?" Macy whispered in confusion.

When he tilted his head and smirked at her, she knew she was a goner. The man was handsome, but he was an absolute god when he smirked.

Chapter Seven
Preacher

Preacher pushed his Harley faster as he flew down the deserted country road. He loved riding on the back roads, and it was one of the reasons he'd chosen to place the clubhouse where he did. Most MC's were found smack dab in the middle of town, but he wanted his away from everything. He loved the peace and quiet of being further out.

But Preacher found riding by himself, just after the sunset, absolute freedom. He loved his club. He made something from nothing. The club had gone through a lot of shit lately, hell the last people to attack had fucking rocket launchers, but they had survived. He was proud as fuck of his brothers, and the woman that loved them, but his passion was riding

Preacher slowed as he took the oncoming turn, then pushed the throttle once more as he hit the last stretch before town. He figured he'd ride straight through, loop around, and head back to the clubhouse. It was dark, but still fairly early, so the streets were deserted. The odd person he passed stopped to wave as he rode by. His club was welcome, and the locals let him know it.

Preacher knew, being president of an MC, he intimidated people. He also knew his many tattoos, worn leather vest and motorcycle didn't help matters. But he figured it was his size that scared them the most. Preacher understood he was a big guy. He was taller than any of the brothers, and he had a shit ton of muscle.

Up ahead he saw a lone figure walking along the sidewalk. He could see right away it was a girl, but something about her caught his interest. He slowed his Harley as he got closer, watching her the entire time. When the girl passed under a street light, he caught right away why he had been so fascinated with her. It was Macy. Snake's sister slowed as she heard his approach, so he parked his bike and called out to her. She turned around, and then her eyes widened as she looked at him.

"Where are you going Hummingbird?" Preacher questioned. Then cursed himself for using the nickname, but it was too late now to take it back. He climbed off his Harley and moved closer to her.

"Hummingbird?" repeated quietly, and he couldn't help but smirk at her.

"Next to my huge ass frame, you're like a tiny Hummingbird," he patiently explained. Preacher then watched in rapt attention as a small, shy smile graced her lips. It made her even prettier.

"I've never had anyone give me a nickname before," Macy admitted. Then she tilted her pretty head. "I like it," she admitted.

If that was how she felt, Preacher would call her fucking Hummingbird from now on. Then something on her forehead caught his attention. He got close, placed his finger under her chin, and turned her face towards the light. A god damned bandage was taped just below her hairline, and blood was dripping from under it.

"What the fuck happened to your head?" he growled in concern.

Macy blinked again, staring at him, then lifted her hand. Preacher looked down to see she held a plastic bag. He let go of her chin and then swore when she looked disappointed. Ignoring how that made him feel, he took the bag and looked inside. Reaching in, he pulled out the broken shower head.

"This is what made that cut on your head?" he asked. Then he watched as she nodded in response.

"It fell off," she whispered.

"So you're headed out to buy a new one?" Preacher asked. Again she simply nodded. The girl was fucking quiet, but he liked that about her.

"Okay," he sighed. "Let's go."

"Uh, what?" Macy asked with a tiny frown.

He looked down at her. "You need a new shower head, the hardware stores about a half block away, let's go," he repeated.

Then Preacher turned, leaving his Harley where it was, and walked. He completely ignored the stunned look she had aimed at him and continued on. He smiled contentedly when he heard her run to catch up. As soon as he reached the door to the store, he stopped her.

"You've got a bit of blood leaking from the bottom of your bandage," Preacher told her. Then he used his free hand to grab the bottom of his tee, lift it up, and dab at the blood. "We'll get your shower head, then I'm taking a good look at that cut," he ordered.

When he held the door open for her, Macy just stood there, and it looked like she was trying to figure him out. Then he watched as she raised her hand, touched her injured head, and blinked up at him again.

Preacher looked up to the sky. The tiny thing looked cute as a button when she blinked at him like that. Fucking complicated he thought, as he watched her finally step into the store.

Chapter Eight
Macy

Macy silently followed the biker through the aisles, as he headed for the plumbing section. She did not understand what was happening, and it completely confused her. He seemed to want to help her, but she had no idea why.

When he stopped, she could only stare at him, as he shuffled through the boxes on the shelves. Suddenly he turned and looked down at her.

"Hummingbird?" Preacher called with a knowing smile. "Are you even listening to me?"

Macy couldn't stop the blush she knew crept across her cheeks. She looked at the ground and shook her head no.

"This one's a good one, and it should last for a long time," he most likely repeated, as he showed her a box.

She ignored everything but the price tag, and she paled at how expensive it was. She immediately took it from him and placed it back on the shelf. Then she squeezed past him so she could see the boxes herself. When she saw one that was priced at ten dollars she snatched it up and grinned.

"This one will work," Macy told him.

Preacher frowned as he studied it, then he shook his head. "That one's crap," he growled. "You'll be lucky if it doesn't break the first time you use it."

She wasn't happy, but she nodded and placed it on the shelf. Scanning again, she grabbed one that was fifteen dollars. She held her breath as he looked at it. He glanced at the price, then he frowned down at her.

"Are you worried about the price?" Preacher questioned, with a look on his face that let her know he was cottoning on to her.

Macy had no idea what to say. She knew if she told the biker she only had thirty dollars in her pocket, he'd get mad. She loved her brother, and she definitely didn't want to make trouble for him.

"I'm only here temporarily," Macy decided to tell him. "I don't need a good one."

"That's true," Preacher admitted. "But you also don't want to have to replace it again."

He again put the box down and picked up another one. She cringed as she looked at the price. This one cost twenty-five dollars, and with tax, she figured it would leave her broke. It was still cheap compared to the rest, but it was still too expensive for her. She dropped her head in defeat and looked to the floor.

"Okay," she whispered, not wanting to upset him.

Immediately Preacher's large hand covered her chin, then he tilted her head up. It surprised her to see an almost tender look on his face.

"I'm buying the shower head," he told her. "I'll take you back, install it, and make sure it works right. Don't worry your pretty little head over something so silly Hummingbird."

Then he let her go, turned, and head to the front of the store. Macy huffed as she watched him walk away. She had to harden her heart, because she knew without a doubt that if she let him in even a little, he'd end up owning hers.

She hurried down the isle and caught up to him just as he was handing the cashier some money. With a nod of thanks, the biker grabbed the bag and headed back outside. She followed him to his bike, then stopped when he climbed on.

"Where are you staying Hummingbird?" he asked.

Macy smiled again at the nickname. Every time he said it her heart beat faster.

"Do you know where the laundromat is?" Macy questioned. He nodded, so she continued. "I'm in the apartment above it."

"Okay, that's not too far. Hop on," he ordered.

"What?" she asked as she eyed the massive bike.

"I'm not leaving my fucking bike, so hop on so we can get this done," he demanded, as he turned and put the bag in a side pouch.

Macy eyed the bike carefully, decided on a good approach, and climbed on. Then she squealed when the biker pulled her close to his back, grabbed her arms, and wrapped them around his heavily muscled stomach.

"Hold on Hummingbird," he ordered with a grin.

Macy did just that with a smile of her own, tightening her arms, and laying her head against his back. She heard him growl, and wasn't sure why, but she didn't move. He told her to hold on, and that's what she was doing.

Chapter Nine
Preacher

Preacher pulled up to the laundromat and parked his Harley. He had mixed feelings about the ride being over. He enjoyed having Macy wrapped around him, but he knew it wasn't right. Even though he felt a pull towards her, he had to put his club first. Then she climbed off and beamed up at him, and he forgot whatever his argument against it was.

"Lead the way Hummingbird," Preached demanded, as he climbed off his bike.

Macy turned away and headed around the side of the building, then climbed a set of stairs. He eyed the stairs in concern and cringed as the first step sagged under his weight. He knew Snake used to stay here, and he immediately wondered how the fuck he made it up and down them. When Preacher reached the top, he actually sighed in relief.

Macy unlocked the door and Preacher followed her inside. He fucking prayed the inside was better than the outside. He almost wanted to close his eyes, because if it was bad, he didn't know what he would do.

When she moved to the couch, and he got a clear view, he looked around. It wasn't as bad as he expected, but it wasn't great either. The place was fucking small, and it was all white. It did however, look clean. Then he heard the loud rumbling noise from downstairs.

"What the fuck is that noise?" Preacher questioned with a frown.

"It's the washing machines," Macy explained. "They run twenty-four hours a day. I'm getting used to them."

Preacher bit his tongue and stomped away, searching for the bathroom. The first door he opened was a bedroom, and he quickly shut the door. All he needed was to get a look at the bed she slept in and fantasize about that. Thankfully the only other door was the bathroom. He stepped inside, then grinned as Macy squeezed in the tight space with him.

Before she could protest, he threw the bag with the shower head in the tub's bottom. Then he grabbed her by the waist, picked her up, and placed her so she was sitting on the counter in front of him.

"Time to look at your head," he growled in explanation. Macy blinked at him again and tilted her head to the side. She was killing him every time she did that, and he knew she had no idea what it did to him.

Preacher slowly raised his hand and peeled off the blood coated bandaid. Then he leaned in to get a better look and smirked knowingly when he heard her breath catch. It was nice to see she was as affected by him as he was by her.

"First aid kit," he ordered.

"I think there's one under the sink," Macy whispered. He bent down, snagged it, and placed it on the counter beside her.

Preacher took an antiseptic wipe and carefully cleaned the cut as best he could. Once done, he was happy to see it actually wasn't that bad. He patched it up, adding antibiotic cream and some butterfly bandages. Satisfied, he kissed the hair just above it then stepped back.

"You got any tools," he questioned. She only stared at him blankly, so he asked, "you okay Hummingbird?"

Macy nodded, fucking blinked again, then answered. "Absolutely." Then as an afterthought stated, "no tools."

"I have some in my bike, I'll be right back."

Preacher turned and took off, braving the stairs once more. When he was at his Harley he paused. He had heard about finding your one from the brothers, and he had a terrible feeling Macy was his.

Preacher shook his head and looked at the laundromat. He wasn't real impressed with the apartment, but it would have to do for now. He grabbed his small tool kit and headed back up the stairs.

When he entered the bathroom again, she was still sitting where he left her. He winked at her, then turned away and got to work. Ten minutes later he was done. He packed up his shit, lifted her down, and headed to the door.

"You got a phone?" Preacher asked. She nodded, without even questioning why he wanted it, and hurried to the kitchen counter.

A minute later she was back and handing him a fucking flip phone. He had to bite his lip to stop from cursing, took it, and programmed his number into it. Then he called himself so he'd have hers. Finally he snapped a quick pic of her, then growled when he saw her head was fucking tilted in the photo. She was definitely killing him.

"You call me if you need me," Preacher ordered gruffly. Then he kissed her head, turned, and walked out the fucking door before he did something stupid.

Chapter Ten
Preacher

Preacher was in a foul mood. He didn't get any fucking sleep, because he kept thinking about his Hummingbird. He hadn't wanted to leave her in the crap apartment with the death trap stairs, but he hadn't had a choice. With Snake being only a prospect, his hands were tied. He sat at the bar in the clubhouse and stared into his glass of whiskey.

"Hey brother," Steele greeted as he clapped him hard on the shoulder and took a seat beside him. Steele nodded to Smoke to indicate he wanted a beer. After the prospect had placed the bottle and moved away, Steele leaned in closer.

"You good?" his VP asked.

"No," Preacher growled back.

"Care to shed some light on why the fuck not?" Steele questioned with a raised brow.

Preacher looked up from the glass, scanned the room to make sure nobody was sitting within hearing distance, and turned to his VP.

"This conversation stays between us," he snarled.

"Always does," Steele reminded him. "Talk to me."

"You know right away Cassie was your one?" Preacher asked.

Steele immediately turned serious. "When I saw her in the restaurant, I felt a strong pull, but I didn't know for sure until I stood beside her and talked to her. I couldn't deny it then."

"What about the other guys?" Preacher pushed.

"Dragon I can't speak for, as he was with Ali before he us. I know Shadow figured out your sister was his the minute he saw her in The Outlaws clubhouse. I also know Trike did too, when he met Misty at the lake the night Carly left her stranded. Like Dragon, Mario and Tripp both knew their girls from before. But Jude fell fast, even though I know the fucker fought it for a long time," Steele smirked.

When Preacher nodded, Steele narrowed his eyes.

"You've found your one," Steele declared, and Preacher dropped his head.

"I fucking have," he sighed. "Girls all I can fucking think about. She's a cute little thing, and I just want to haul her close and protect her from the world."

Steele chuckled. "Fucking poet," he snorted. "You know you're fucked right?"

"I hear you brother," Preacher growled. "I don't have the time or the room for this shit in my life. I have a fucking MC to run. I'm the god damned president, my head needs to stay with the club. If I fuck up, or get distracted, brothers will get hurt."

Steele's face turned to a mask of fury. "You fucking think the girls make us weak? Do I look weak to you?" When Preacher eyed him in surprise, Steele continued. "The girls make us fucking stronger. I love my brothers, and I love this club, but my Little Mouse gives me something to fight for. She's mine, and she depends on me to keep her safe. It means I need to be stronger, and tougher, so I can do that. Fucking weak my ass," Steele huffed.

"I don't know whether I'm ready for all that," Preacher admitted.

"Well you better fucking figure it out," Steele ordered. "The way things go around here, she's either already in trouble, or will be soon. Us fuckers never get our girls without a fucking fight."

When Preacher just glared at him, Steele narrowed his eyes.

"Fuck me," Steele growled. "She's already in trouble."

Preacher didn't bother to deny it.

"Bad?" Steele pushed.

"Bad enough," Preacher replied.

"You need help?" Steele demanded.

Preacher looked down at his glass, then lifted it to his mouth and took a healthy swig. "Not yet, but I have a feeling that will change."

"Right, well don't wait too long grandpa, because things move fast around here."

Preacher glared at his VP. "I'm twenty-seven, that's only a year older than you fucker. You need me to take you outside and teach you some manners," he growled.

Steele busted out laughing. "No thank you. I was taught early on to respect my elders." Then the ass jumped from the stool before Preacher could grab him and took off.

"Fucking bikers," Preacher grumbled as he downed the last of his whiskey.

Then he turned and found Mario headed his way.

"Got a minute?" Mario asked.

"Definitely," Preacher immediately responded. Then he turned and headed for a table Mario stopped at. He wasn't surprised to see Trent headed their way, and Steele turning back to join them. It was time to get some answers.

Chapter Eleven
Macy

Macy trudged up the stairs after her third exhausting day at work. She had hoped that as the days went by, the job would get easier, but it was only getting worse. She was sore everywhere, and she was so exhausted, she had no idea how she was still standing. Macy decided Mrs. Tang was a child of the devil. She didn't understand how one tiny Chinese woman could be so cruel. The lady yelled all the time.

Reaching the top step, Macy unlocked the door and headed inside. She literally stripped on the way to the bathroom, dropping her clothes where they fell. She stepped on the thin bath mat and started the shower. As soon as she had the water steaming hot, she climbed inside and pulled the curtain shut.

The shower head worked amazing, and it was so much better than the old one. She had no idea how to thank Preacher, but she knew she was in his debt. She didn't know what she'd been thinking, heading out on her own to buy one. Firstly, she had no tools to assemble the stupid thing with. And secondly, she wouldn't know how to install it anyway. Preacher had been a godsend.

Macy stayed in the shower until the water ran cold, then sighed in agitation and reluctantly climbed out. She hurriedly dried off, towel dried her hair, and braided it damp. Then she padded across the hall to her bedroom and got dressed. She eyed the bed longingly, but figured if she went to bed hungry she'd wake up starving.

Heading to the kitchen, Macy eyed her cupboards. Ramen noodles and peanut butter stared back at her, and she had to look away. After eating them for the past several days, she wanted something different. Sighing, she moved to the stash of money she had left and pulled out a ten. It was probably being reckless, but she really wanted a burger, and she remembered there was a fast food place around the corner.

Decision made, Macy shoved the bill in her pocket and headed out. She took her time walking to the take-out restaurant, she was just too tired to go any faster, and it was a nice evening. Once there she pushed the door open and headed inside. Just her luck, there was a huge line up, so she figured she'd be there a while.

Macy studied the line and realized there was a huge biker near the front. She knew if she tried to leave, he'd probably see her anyway, so she looked to the floor and stayed where she was.

A minute later she heard him curse and looked up to see her brother staring down at her. She froze at the frustrated look on his face, knowing she should have bolted the minute she saw him. When he turned back around and cruelly ignored her, she looked back down at the floor sadly.

A minute later his food was ready, and Macy watched warily as he approached with two bags. She was shocked when he stopped right beside her. Looking up, she couldn't mask the sadness at seeing him. He shoved a bag into her arms, and she was forced to grab it before it fell.

"You got a job at the laundromat yet?" Snake growled. Macy nodded up at him in reply as she held the bag to her chest. "Good. You get paid yet?"

She shook her head no and looked to the floor again. Then she heard him sigh in frustration as he reached into his pocket, pulled out a couple bills, and shoved them in her free hand. Without a word he turned and strode towards the door.

"Thank you," Macy whispered. She didn't think she said it very loud, but he stopped at the door and turned. He studied her intensely for a minute, then frowned and walked out.

She waited a minute, and when she heard his Harley pull out she left herself. When she reached her tiny apartment she hurried up the stairs and let herself inside. Setting her food down, Macy finally opened her hand, and was surprised to see two tens in it. That meant she now had fifty dollars.

When her stomach growled, she opened the bag and dug into her food. It was the best burger ever, and that was just because her big brother bought it for her.

Chapter Twelve
Preacher

Preacher sat at the table and nodded in thanks to Smoke as he placed a new glass of whiskey in front of him. With the way things were going, he figured he'd need it. Mario, Trent and Steele sat too, and then he wasn't surprised when Dragon, Navaho and Jude pulled up chairs and joined them.

"Is this something we need to discuss in church?" Jude questioned as he eyed the other brothers.

"Not yet," Preacher answered, "but that may change once I hear what Mario has to say. Where the fucks Snake?" he growled, as he surveyed the room.

Steele reached in his pocket, pulled out his cell, and made a call. "He's just pulling up to the gate now."

"This about the trouble his fathers in?" Dragon asked as he reached for his beer and took a long drag.

"Yep," Preacher replied. "If troubles coming, I want to be prepared."

"Oh, we're prepared," Dagger smirked, as he twisted a chair around backwards and straddled it. "I put the rocket launchers and grenades from Jude's fiasco in my room."

"Jesus Christ," Jude snarled. "Shouldn't you lock them up or something?"

"They're in my closet. And I've got a combination lock on the door," Dagger happily informed them.

"Oh well, that's okay then," Jude snorted sarcastically.

Preacher sighed. "Get them out of your room and store them with the rest of the fucking weapons," he furiously ordered.

Dagger pouted, but he did so nodding. "Should have kept my mouth shut," he muttered.

Finally Snake stepped in and headed their way. Once he was seated Preacher looked at Mario and signalled with a flick of his wrist to start.

"Trent and Nick did quite a bit of digging and came up pretty lucky. Based on Wes' address, the biggest loan shark in the area is a guy named Pike," Mario explained.

"Shit," Snake cursed. "I went to school with the guy. He's a real nasty fucker. His father used to beat him, and word is when Pike turned fourteen he took a fucking crow bar to him. Bashed his head in. Since then there's been at least five murders that the local cops know he's responsible for, but can't pin on him."

"Right," Mario confirmed. "His last girlfriend also disappeared. No one's seen or heard from her in five months. Word is, Pike doesn't seem at all bothered by it."

"So how much does Wes owe?" Dagger questioned.

"I couldn't get an exact number, but rumour is it's in the fifty thousand dollar range," Trent told them.

"Fuck," Dragon cursed. "That's a shit ton of coin."

"I made some calls to a couple local contacts, and they asked around," Mario continued. "Looks like Pike's been sniffing around your sister for a long time. Apparently she wants nothing to do with him."

"Yeah, he tried to get in her pants in high school too, but I shut that shit down," Snake growled.

Preacher turned to face him in surprise. "I thought you hated her?" he asked with a raised brow.

"She's still my fucking sister," Snake sneered in response.

"So you knocked some sense into him?" Steele pushed Snake.

"I did," Snake told him. "He may be meaner, but I'm fucking bigger."

"So he couldn't have her back then, what's to say he didn't set your dad up to take a heavy hit at the tables. Maybe force his hand," Jude declared, and Preacher had to agree with him.

"Right," Dragon continued. "Get the girl another way. He know's your dad can't pay the debt and offers a solution."

"But he had to know dad would take her and run?" Snake countered. "He may be an ass, but he'd never hand Macy over."

"So how do we know the fucker didn't have Wes followed here?" Navaho asked, finally adding his two cents.

"We don't," Preacher sighed. "But it's been about five days, and there's been no sign of him that we know of. My guess, if he knew where she was, he wouldn't waste time coming after her."

"So we can't go after him yet?" Dagger huffed.

"Not unless we want retribution," Preacher replied. "But the minute he steps foot around here, he's as good as dead," he growled.

"So you're getting the club involved in this?" Steele inquired with a raised brow.

"Damn right," Preacher decided. "The loan may not be our concern, and Snake isn't a patched in member yet, but I'm not letting a murderer show up and start trouble."

"Okay," Steele agreed with a menacing grin. "Let's make a plan."

Chapter Thirteen
Preacher

"I think this needs to continue in church," Preacher finally declared. "If we got this fucker headed our way with kidnapping and destruction on his mind, we need the entire club in the loop. I want everyone here that can be here in ten minutes."

Snake immediately piped up. "It involves my family, I need to be included."

"And you're not a fucking patched member," Preacher growled to put the prospect in his place. "After church, you and me can have a sit down. I'll let you know what we've decided. You won't be left in the dark. I also want to discuss a few things with you anyway, so we'll get that done too."

Snake knew not to argue, so Preacher shook his head at the pissed off prospect. Snake finally nodded and left the table.

"He going to be a problem?" Mario questioned in concern.

"He better not be," Preacher snarled. He downed his whiskey in one gulp, let the burn fester, then headed to the room they held church in.

Exactly ten minutes later, the room was full. Smoke and Snake were left in the common room, and Doc volunteered to man the gates. Mario also had a couple of his men show up to help keep an eye out while they were busy.

Preacher started by laying out everything he knew. Once he was done, and the brothers were up to speed, he let them speak up.

"So we're backing prospects now?" Shadow asked with a bite to his words.

"No, we're protecting the club and the town that relies on us," Preacher declared. Shadow nodded in acceptance.

"So we bring the girl in?" Raid suggested.

"We can't," Preacher sighed. "Snake isn't a fully patched member, and the girl isn't claimed."

"What's she look like?" Dagger immediately asked.

"Not fucking happening," Preacher growled without thought.

"But if I claimed her, the problems solved," Dagger said with a grin.

"You make a move on her, I'll shove my foot up your ass," Preacher vowed.

"Uh, someone's in a mood," Dagger huffed as he crossed his massive arms. "You claiming her yourself?"

Preacher sighed, knowing he needed to be honest with his club.

"Not yet," he admitted, as he eyed the brothers around the table. "I've met her fucking twice." Then he turned to Shadow. "Plus we have rules about brothers dating other members sisters."

"Yep," Shadow instantly agreed. "Unless you want the five hits like I took. I'd say I got off easy though, I'd fucking die for my baby girl."

"So she's your one?" Trike questioned, looking like he was ready to celebrate.

"Definitely," Preacher replied. "But right now she's safe where she is, and until I claim her, that where she needs to be."

"So what if we patch Snake in?" Raid asked. "His time as a prospect should be done soon."

"The guy needs an attitude adjustment first," Steele growled. "Fucker can't be a part of this family if he can't even look after his own. He treats his sister like shit, and I don't want him patched in until he changes."

"Agreed," Preacher declared. "So until then we put a brother on her twenty-four seven, and we give Darren and Colin a call and let them know what's going down. They can probably get us more intel on Pike too."

"Sounds good," Steele agreed. "How long you plan on fighting the pull for?"

Preacher glared at his VP. "I'm putting the club first like I always do. It's a big fucking step, and I want to make damn sure I'm not making a mistake."

Jude snickered from the end of the table. "Yeah, good luck with that. The pull is hard to ignore. The more you deny it, the crazier you get. Plus my rainbow almost blew up before I accepted it. Fucking gutted me."

Preacher hung his head. The thought of anything happening to his Hummingbird gutted him too.

"I hear you," he said. "Let me deal with Snake and wrap my head around this, and then I'll fucking pull her in."

"Pull her in fucking quick," Tripp advised. "Our track records shit."

"So we're building another cabin," Dagger questioned with a frown.

"Do I look like the fucking cabin type?" Preacher sneered.

"It grows on you," Shadow promised.

"Well nothings fucking growing on me," Preacher growled as he threw back the last of his whiskey.

"So she'll be living in your tiny fucking room?" Dragon snickered.

Preacher frowned, knowing with certainty that wouldn't work. Shit, he thought, now what the fuck was he going to do with her?

Chapter Fourteen
Preacher

Once church was over, Preacher grabbed Snake and headed for his office. Steele raised his brow in a silent question, but Preacher shook his head. This chat needed to be between just the two of them.

When Snake entered the office Preacher slammed the door, walked around his desk, and sat. He motioned to the chair on the opposite side of the desk, and Snake reluctantly sat too. By the look on the prospects face, he was more than ready to do battle.

"First things first," Preacher stated. "I'm the fucking president of this club. You can speak your mind, but don't fucking disrespect me. I know you're pissed and I know you have quite a bit to say, but keep that in mind, because I have no problem cutting your fucking ass from this club."

Preacher glared at the prospect for a minute, silently daring him to say something. When he remained silent, Preacher continued.

"First thing I want to ask, is if you've thought about the place you left your sister in?" he demanded.

Snake immediately scowled. "I lived there for over a year. There's nothing fucking wrong with it. It's small, but it's clean and it's warm."

Preacher raised his hand. "It's shit, and it's over a fucking laundromat."

"Fine," Snake grumbled. "But it's all I got." Preacher gave him that and nodded.

"How much money does she have?" he asked next. "She didn't look like she came with much, and with Wes owing money, I doubt he had any to give her."

"I gave her sixty when I dropped her off, and another thirty when I saw her yesterday," Snake replied. "Is this really any of your business?" he growled.

Preacher sighed. "So she's been there almost a week. I'm assuming she had to buy groceries and shit." Snake nodded, and he continued. "And basic things like bathroom supplies." When he paused, the prospect nodded again. "That's not much money. What about rent?"

Snake sat up straighter and seemed to get angrier. "It's paid until next week, and she's got a fucking job. I'm a god damned prospect. Only patched members get a cut. Prospects get shit. I earn a bit from working on the cars and that's it. I had an apartment I signed a lease on. I had to pay the rent until the lease was over. I have a fucking bike that keeps breaking down. And I'm still paying for the damn thing. I gave her everything I could spare."

Snake eyed Preacher carefully. "You always this curious about prospects? Seems you're digging a little too deep," he sneered. Then Snake leaned forward as he considered something and placed his hands on the desk. "How the fuck do you know where I left her?"

"It's my fucking job to know," Preacher growled. "With the possibility of Pike bringing trouble our way, I need to know everything."

"I understand that," Snake admitted. "But you're taking an awful interest in my sister."

"And you don't fucking give a shit about her?" Preacher accused.

"I hate her," Snake agreed. "But I fucking love her too," he sneered.

"Fucking explain that?" Preacher sighed in aggravation.

"You know what loosing your mother does to you at such a young age?" Snake asked, but he continued without waiting for an answer. "It god damned guts you. Then I had a father that couldn't cope, and a newborn to live with. My mother had cancer, and she stopped the radiation when she got pregnant. She chose Macy over herself. So yeah, I was pissed."

"So you grow a set of balls and get over it," Preacher growled.

"I wasn't finished," Snake growled back. "Macy was home about a month when she got sick. Turned into pneumonia fucking fast. Doctors said she was too young to fight it, and there wasn't anything they could do. It was like loosing my mother all over again. She suddenly got better, doctors couldn't explain it, said it was a fucking miracle. To this day, if she gets a cold, it turns bad fast. She's had to be damn careful, and she's been back to the hospital three times."

Preacher stared at the prospect, not sure what to say. He decided it was best to let him get it out, so he nodded to continue.

"My dads a jerk. My sister though is an angel. I lost my mom, and it gutted me. I lose her, it will fucking end me. So you live with that on your chest and see how you deal with it. You think I treat her like shit, well I still look out for her, I just keep my fucking distance," Snake told him.

Preacher watched as Snake stood and headed for the door. "I got a car to work on in the shop. We done?" he questioned. Preacher nodded, and the prospect walked out.

It turned out Preacher had a lot more to fix then he thought.

Chapter Fifteen
Macy

Macy went to work the next morning in a much better mood. With the burger in her tummy, she had slept better, and she felt better than she usually did. She smiled when she thought of her brother buying it for her. He hated her, yet he had done something nice for her. She didn't want to hope, or analyze it too much, but it was hard not to.

Macy arrived downstairs at the laundromat five minutes early and immediately headed to the back. When Mrs. Tang noticed her, she stomped over.

"You five minutes late," she yelled. Stunned, Macy checked her watch.

"I'm five minutes early," she whispered in confusion.

"Your watch wrong. You five minutes late. I dock your pay," Mrs. Tang yelled. "Get to work."

Macy sighed and walked over to the large steamers. She hit a button to heat the machines up and moved over to the huge pile of clothes. She learned it was way easier if she sorted them first. When the clothes came out of the steamers, she could fold them and stack them quicker.

She took twenty minutes to sort everything, and by that time the steamers were hot. The room was already pretty hot, and she was sweating before she'd even really started. Dropping her head, she picked up a pile of clothes and got to work.

Four hours later it was time for lunch. Macy left the machines on, like she always did, and headed out the door. Mrs. Tang gave her twenty minutes for lunch, and she used every minute. She left out a side door and headed around back.

When she got to the stairs, she stopped cold. The big biker she was quickly becoming fascinated with, was standing at the bottom. In his hand was a paper bag, and it looked like he'd been waiting a bit.

"Heard you got a job. Brought tacos," he smirked. She couldn't help but smile at the biker.

"I love tacos," Macy admitted quietly.

"Jesus, you're pretty when you smile," he said. Then before she could respond, he grabbed her hand and dragged her up the rickety stairs.

She passed him the key when they reached the top, and he unlocked the door and walked inside.

"Is it wrong I'm always surprised when I make it to the top of those fucking things?" he said with a scowl.

Macy didn't know how to respond, so she headed to the kitchen to get a couple plates and some napkins. When she turned to head back, she squealed when she bumped into him. For a big guy he was awfully quiet.

She was shocked when he pushed past her, opened her cupboards, and nosed around. She cringed at the four packets of noodles and jar of peanut butter that were sitting there. When he moved to the fridge and found only a bottle of orange juice, she waited anxiously for his anger.

"Hummingbird," he quietly called as he turned worried eyes towards her. "You know this isn't good."

"My brother bought me a burger last night," she whispered.

Suddenly the biker moved, and she found herself pushed up against the counter as he crowded her in. She stared at his vest and was surprised to see the word Preacher stitched on a patch.

"Your names Preacher?" she asked in surprise, as she reached up and touched the patch.

"Fuck me," he growled, as he placed his thumb on her chin and tilted her head up to look at him. "You didn't know my name?"

"You never told me, and Snake just grunts at me," Macy explained.

"Shit," he said. "I'm fucking this up, and I haven't even started yet."

Macy had no idea what he was talking about, so she tilted her head and blinked at him. As soon as she did he growled, then he slammed his mouth down on hers. She was shocked for a minute, but his lips were soft, and it was something she'd been dreaming about for a while. She immediately leaned into him and kissed him back. The kiss didn't last long before he was pulling back, but it was everything she dreamed it would be.

"Real names Timothy, but I fucking hate it. You can call me anything you want, but don't fucking call me that," Preacher ordered.

"Stud muffin," she whispered without thinking. She slammed her hand over her mouth and watched nervously as his eyes narrowed on her for a minute. Then he threw back his head and laughed.

Chapter Sixteen
Preacher

Preacher couldn't help but throw his head back and laugh. His Hummingbird calling him stud muffin was fucking funny. He couldn't remember when the last time was he laughed that hard. Daggers antics made him chuckle sometimes, and the way Lucy and Klutz went at each other was comical, but no one brought out a full laugh in him. He smiled down at his girl, while she stood stock still and watched him.

"I like when you laugh," she whispered after he got control of himself.

"I like it too Hummingbird," Preacher admitted. "Now I know you're on lunch, so let's eat and talk a bit before you need to get back."

Macy nodded and followed him over to the couch. He opened the bag, put two tacos on her plate, and four on his own. She blinked at him, but didn't say a word.

"You doing okay at the laundromat?" he asked.

She swallowed and nodded quickly, then looked back down at her plate. He immediately narrowed his eyes at her. Macy was lying, but he wasn't sure how to proceed. With his temper, it might be best to check up on her a bit more before he jumped the gun.

"Would it be okay if I came back over tonight? Maybe brought some Chinese. We could watch a movie or some tv?" he asked.

"You want to come back tonight?" Macy questioned in obvious surprise. "Aren't you busy doing president stuff?"

Preacher had his taco halfway to his mouth when she said that, and he was glad he hadn't taken a bite. He chuckled as he turned to face her.

"President stuff?" he smirked.

Macy looked down at her plate shyly. "I just figured you had rides to plan, bad guys to take out, and guns to clean."

Preacher busted out laughing again. "You watch a lot of Sons of Anarchy?" he questioned.

"It's a good show," she whispered defensively.

"I'm not knocking your choice in shows Hummingbird, I'm just laughing at your comparison," he explained.

"I don't understand," she admitted.

"We're a bit different from their club," Preacher told her. "We don't do anything illegal unless it's warranted, and we mostly just work on cars and bikes. Our free time is our own, so we drink and hang out."

"What would warrant the illegal stuff?" she questioned curiously. He sighed not surprised that was what she picked up on.

"We protect our own," Preacher explained. "If someone in our club, or someone one of us cares about is in trouble, we do what needs to be done to fix it. Sometimes the lines between legal and illegal get a bit blurred."

"So that's why you're here?" Macy frowned sadly. "Because I'm Snake's sister and I may be in trouble. But Snake doesn't care about me, so technically I'm not the clubs problem."

Preacher absolutely lost it when she said that. "First of all," he growled angrily. "Me and your brother had a chat, he cares about you, he's just being an ass. And second of all, I'm not here because of your family ties to one of my prospects."

"Then why are you here?" she questioned.

"Because you got my attention the minute you stepped out of that fucking car. You're adorable, you're strong, and I'm drawn to you. You make me want to know everything about you, and you make me want to hold on to you and protect you from the fucking world," Preacher admitted.

Tears instantly fell from her eyes and he glared at them. "I've scared you," he said. "I've never cared about anyone before, and I'm not good at expressing it."

"No," she quickly denied, as she swiped at her tears with the back of her hand. "I think you said it perfectly. All I've ever wanted was for someone to hold me. I've waited my whole life for a man to say those words to me, thinking it would never happen."

Preacher moved quickly then, scooping her up and placing her on his lap. He wrapped his arms around her and held on tight. She gripped his shirt and buried her tear streaked face in his neck. He thought of Snake and knew he'd have to deal with that, but right now he didn't care.

"You know, maybe stud muffin was a bit premature. I think cuddle bunny might be better," his girl muffled into his neck.

"Fuck," he said as he held her tighter. He knew his 'figuring shit out' idea was crap. Now he just needed to go tell the club he was claiming her.

Chapter Seventeen
Macy

Preacher stayed for another few minutes and they talked and cuddled some more. It surprised Macy at how easy it was to be around the big biker. He made her feel comfortable, and that was completely new to her. She was reluctant to move, but she couldn't be late getting back to the laundromat.

He followed her as she locked up and helped her down the rickety stairs. When he reached the bottom he pulled her close, and she found herself in heaven once more. He surprised her by kissing her, then he let go and gave her a gentle shove in the direction of the side door.

"I'll see you tonight Hummingbird," Preacher promised.

Macy smiled at him shyly. She figured something would probably come up to cause him to cancel, but still nodded to please him. Once inside, she turned back and watched as he climbed on his bike and rode away. She stayed in the same spot until she could no longer see him.

"Why you just stand there?" Mrs. Tang yelled. "Get back to work. You late anyway. I dock your pay."

Macy turned and looked at the clock, then down at her watch. This time there was a ten minute difference. Either Mrs. Tang was changing the clock and messing with her, or her watch wasn't working right. She had a funny feeling her watch wasn't the problem.

Two hours later Macy was sweating again. She looked at the clock and knew she still had an hour left, but she was exhausted. She sighed and wiped the sweat from her brow as she pulled the last pair of pants out of the steamer. She carefully folded the hot garment and added them to the top of the pile of the ones already done.

Macy turned to the pile of shirts and carefully started feeding them through the steamers. Slowly but steadily the pile started to go down. She was half way through when Mrs. Tang showed up again.

"You too slow. You should have everything done," her boss yelled. Then she pointed to the pile of blouses that Macy hadn't gotten too yet. "You do them too."

Macy looked at her watch and realized her shift was almost over. She looked at Mrs. Tang's furious expression and sighed.

"My shift ends in ten minutes. I really don't think I'm going to get all that done in the time I have left," Macy explained.

"You finish. Work until they done. Stay until they done," Mrs. Tang ordered as she pointed a finger at her threateningly. "But no more money. You learn to do work on time."

Macy shook her head. "I have plans, and I don't want to work longer if you won't pay me."

Mrs. Tang squinted her eyes then headed her way. Macy immediately took a step back, almost afraid of the tiny angry woman. Mrs. Tang reached over and picked up a large metal ruler off a table as she kept coming.

Again Macy took another step back, not realizing how close she was to the steamer rollers. When her back hit the hot roller, she screamed in pain. She jumped forward, but she knew it was too late, as she immediately felt the skin on her back burning. She cried in pain as she fell forward and tried to pull the tee she was wearing away.

"Get out," Mrs. Tang bellowed. "You try to break my steamer. You fired."

Macy actually stared at the woman in shock for a minute. Then she turned and fled as the tears fell furiously down her cheeks. She rushed up the stairs and hurried inside her tiny apartment, terrified she would pass out from the pain.

Because the burn was on her back, Macy couldn't see it, and she couldn't reach it. She panicked for a few minutes, and then her eyes caught on the cell phone laying on the counter. She snagged it and hit the only button she had programmed.

"Hummingbird," Preacher greeted. "You couldn't wait until tonight to talk to me?"

Macy tried to talk, but she only ended up crying harder. She was in pain, she was hysterical, and she needed him.

"Where are you?" Preacher yelled into the phone harshly, and she knew he understood something was wrong.

"The apartment," she choked out through her tears. "It hurts," she managed tell him. She heard a motorcycle starting up in the background, and then he was yelling again.

"You hold tight baby, I'm on my way," he promised.

Chapter Eighteen
Preacher

Preacher lost his fucking mind when he hung up the phone. His Hummingbird was hurt, and she sounded broken. He had no idea what happened, but his gut told him it was bad. Through the years he'd learned to trust his gut, so he knew he needed to get to his girl fast. If Pike was there, he'd fucking end him.

He was already astride his Harley and was ready to pull out, when he noticed Snake come out of the garage. Immediately he flagged the prospect over, happy when Snake jogged his way. Snake took one look at his face and tensed.

"What's wrong?" he questioned.

"Macy," Preacher growled. "I need you to find Doc and get him to her apartment."

"What the fuck happened to her?" Snake yelled.

"Don't know and don't have time for this. I need to get to her. She called, didn't sound good," Preacher hurried to say.

"She called you?" Snake roared furiously.

"You didn't leave your fucking number," Preached roared back. "And I'm fucking claiming her. You got a problem with that, we'll duke it out later."

Then he left Snake standing there with his face etched in fury and pulled away. As he rode through the gate, he saw Snake finally run back to the clubhouse. He turned onto the road and gunned it, then wasn't surprised when four bikes pulled up beside him.

Preacher nodded at Steele in thanks and pushed his Harley faster. It took him and his brothers ten minutes to reach the laundromat. He barely had the bike turned off, before he was climbing off and charging for the stairs. They groaned and swayed under his weight, but he didn't have time to worry about it. He shoved open the door, stepped inside, and froze. He heard his brothers cursing behind him.

His poor Hummingbird was lying on the floor on her stomach. She was crying quietly and had a pillow clutched to her chest. Her back was completely exposed, and it looked like her tee had been burned right off her.

Preacher roared in fury as he tore across the room. He dropped to his knees and pulled her onto his lap, careful not to touch her back.

"Jesus Hummingbird, what the fuck happened?" Preacher asked as he tried to gentle his voice.

Macy tilted her head and looked at his brothers, who had crowded close, then leaned back to look at him.

"I burned it on the steamers at the laundromat," she painfully whispered.

Dragon dropped to his knees as well and got close, capturing her attention.

"Honey, can you explain how this happened?" he asked her gently.

She looked at Dragon and more tears fell. "Mrs. Tang was mad. She came at me and I stepped back."

Preacher's body locked solid. "She came at you?" he asked carefully, not even trying to hide his rage.

"She doesn't like me much," Macy told them. "I was worried she'd hit me with the ruler."

Dragon's eyes flew to him and then turned cold. Immediately he was on his feet, with Steele and Dagger following him. Raid stayed close and was trying to get a look at Macy's back.

"No," Preacher roared, and his brothers immediately stopped. "I'm going to be a part of that conversation, and I can't fucking do that now. Macy needs us."

Steele nodded. "I'll call Doc and make sure Snake found him. We need a vehicle, and Doc usually brings his."

Preacher nodded, then turned to Raid. "What can we do?" he questioned, knowing the brother had medical training.

"Honestly, I don't fucking know. It's a bad burn, and I can treat that, but she's bleeding where it broke the skin. I'd suggest getting her under a cold shower, but make sure the water is a really fucking gentle spray. We need to clean it and stop the burn so Doc can see what he's working with," Raid explained.

"Right," Preacher agreed. Then he scooped his girl up awkwardly, holding her at the neck and under the knees.

"I'll get the water the right temperature," Raid said, as he hurried ahead of him. "Dagger find some scissors or a sharp knife."

"I've got a decent pocket knife in my vest," Dagger replied as he followed.

Then Preacher was sitting on the counter as Raid started the water. His Hummingbird was on his lap, with her back faced out. Dagger handed Raid the knife then stepped out of the way. It was time to get a better look at the damage.

Chapter Nineteen
Macy

Macy held onto Preacher tightly as Raid approached with Dagger's pocket knife. She saw the biker called Dragon approach her side, so she twisted to look at him.

"Hey Macy. I'm going to lift the bottom of your tee and pull it slowly away from your skin. It will make it easier for Raid to cut. There's some blood on it where it was burned away, so it may hurt a bit, but we'll be careful," Dragon soothingly explained.

Macy turned back to Preacher and stared into his dark eyes. He didn't smile or reassure her, but his eyes were intense as he watched her in concern. She felt her shirt lift, and then she heard the sound of her shirt tearing. It wasn't too bad, until he hit the spot where it was stuck. Pain shot up her spine, and tears started to stream down her face.

"God dammit," Preacher yelled. "You're fucking hurting her. Stop."

"No," Macy whispered. "It's okay, and I know it needs to be done. Keep going." She tried to smile through her pain, but she knew she wasn't successful when he growled.

After a minute she knew the shirt had been sliced all the way through. She pulled away from Preacher and let it fall to his lap.

"Towel," Preacher demanded. Immediately a towel landed in his hand. "Do the fucking bra too if you have too. Just give me a second to cover her."

Macy watched, as thankfully all the men turned away. Preacher threw the tee on the floor, then maneuvered the towel between them. She looked down to see it completely covered her front.

"Thank you," she whispered.

"I've got you Hummingbird," Preacher assured her. "You'll always be comfortable when I'm around."

Then Raid was back, and the bra was undone. Preacher carefully slipped it off her shoulders and pulled it away from her. Then that too was thrown on the floor.

"Okay," Raid said. "I've got the temperature on the shower good, but the sprays too strong. I'm afraid this may do more damage than help."

"Not if I can fucking help it," Preacher snarled. Then he stood and carefully placed her on her feet. When she swayed Raid grabbed her arm and steadied her. She watched in silence as Preacher began to strip. Once everything was off but his boxers, he stepped into the spray, and blocked most with his large body.

"Fucking genius," Dragon smirked, as they heard voices in the living room.

Suddenly Snake pushed into the small bathroom, with an older man following. He took one look at her and lost it.

"Why the fuck are you in a bathroom half naked with a bunch of bikers?" Snake bellowed. "And what the fuck are you doing?" he growled at Preacher.

Macy looked at her brother, as more tears fell from her face. "My back hurts," she whispered. "They're helping me."

Snake's face turned into a mask of fury. "Turn the fuck around," he ordered.

Macy turned to face Preacher, not knowing what to do.

"Don't fucking look at him," her brother growled. "Turn the fuck around." Slowly, with Raid's help, she did as asked and turned so he had a good view of her back.

"Mother fucker," Snake hissed, then she heard a crash and Preacher was yelling.

Macy spun around to see Dragon and Raid both had a hold of Snake. He was thrashing and trying to get to her.

"Snake," she cried through her tears. Immediately he stopped thrashing and glared at the bikers with a look that promised murder.

"Let me go," Snake ordered. The bikers looked to Preacher before they set Snake free. Macy could do nothing but watch as he stalked towards her. When he was close, he reached up and brushed at her tears with his thumbs. "When I find out who did this, I'm going to fucking end them," he vowed.

Then she was carefully pulled into his arms. She couldn't remember ever being held by him, and it was absolute heaven.

"I'm so fucking sorry," Snake cried as he held her to his chest.

"We need to clean her back," Doc quietly interrupted. "I need to see it."

"Everybody out," Snake yelled. Then he turned to Doc. "I'm helping."

Macy watched as the bikers left, then it was just the four of them.

"Get her in the tub and under that spray," Doc ordered.

Snake nodded, and then she was lifted into the tub. Preacher held her shoulders, but she still swayed. The next thing she knew, her brother climbed into the tub fully dressed, and she was cradled against his massive chest. Preacher blocked most of the spray, but she didn't feel a thing. All she felt was the warmth of Snake's arms as he held her.

Chapter Twenty
Preacher

Preacher blocked the spray of water as he got a good look at his Hummingbirds back. He wasn't a doctor, but he knew it was bad. He could hear her quiet sobs, as she rested her forehead on her brother's chest. Snake still didn't have a clue what happened, and Preacher knew he'd have to fill the prospect in soon.

"It's not as bad as it looks," Doc informed them, as he peered closely at her back and studied it. "She'll definitely need a couple stitches, but I think all it will take is a lot of ointment and a lot of rest. We'll need to keep it covered and clean, but it should heal with minimal scarring. Of course it will be uncomfortable for a while," he told them.

"How the fuck did this happen?" Snake growled, as he kissed his sister's head.

"She was working downstairs," Preacher explained. "Got too close to a steamer."

Snake narrowed his eyes at him. "You leaving something out?"

"Yep, and I'll be more than happy to fill you in once we get Macy sorted," Preacher told Snake.

"She's starting to shiver bad," Snake said in concern.

"Time to get out Hummingbird," Preacher decided. Then he lifted her under the arms and placed her on the bath mat. He stepped out behind her and grabbed a dry towel.

"Turn for me baby," he ordered. She did, and he gently dried her arms and hair as best he could. Snake climbed out, dripping water everywhere, and held Macy so she wouldn't fall.

"I need to get these wet pants off her," Preacher sighed. "Why don't you take your soggy ass out of here and find her some loose sweats or pyjama pants."

Snake glared at Preacher, then finally nodded. "I'll be right back," he told Macy, then he was out the door.

Before Preacher could make a move, the door opened again, and someone shoved a huge ass blanket inside.

"I know you're claiming her, and we will definitely be discussing that, but cover her the fuck up," Snake growled. Then pyjama pants hit him in the face.

Preacher actually chuckled. For a guy that hated his sister and never showed her a hint of love, he was awfully protective. He looked at his Hummingbird, to see her staring at the door in awe.

"Things are going to change now Hummingbird," Preacher told her. "And I can guarantee the changes will be good ones."

Macy looked at him and nodded, then reached for the zipper of her jeans. Thankfully Doc had turned away. Preacher dropped down and peeled the wet pants down her legs, then eyed her wet underwear. She saw what he was looking at and nodded. He tugged at the wet towel she was still using to cover her chest, and it hung low enough, that it now covered all of her. He tore her underwear off and threw them in the corner.

"Okay baby, let go of the wet towel and replace it with this dry one, Preacher instructed as he shut his eyes. When she was done, he helped her into the dry pyjama pants, and asked her to turn. Then he wrapped the blanket around her front, leaned against the counter, and pulled her into his chest.

"You better let Snake back in here before you start," Preacher told Doc. Doc nodded and headed for the door. A minute later Snake was back in the room.

"The quicker this is stitched the better," Doc explained. "I can give her a needle to numb the area, and we can do it right here."

"Fucking guts me," Snake growled, not even trying to hide the pain he was feeling. Then he narrowed his eyes at Preacher. "Can you get fucking dressed?" he sneered.

Preacher nodded and let go of Macy. Then he moved to his clothes. "Fine, but don't touch her. I just got her dry and your wet and most likely cold."

"She's my sister," Snake angrily declared.

"And she's my one," Preacher growled back.

Snake immediately took a step back. "Fuck me," he complained. "It just had to be my sister."

"I'll protect her with my life," Preacher vowed sincerely. "She'll never know a day without my love and tenderness."

Snake turned to Doc. "Let's get this god damned over with. I need to rip apart whoever did this, then I need to get rip-roaring drunk."

Chapter Twenty One
Macy

Macy held tight to Preacher as Doc stitched her up. She kept her eyes tightly closed, and her face buried in his chest. Her back still hurt, but the stitches themselves didn't, thanks to the needle Doc had given her. Snake made sure she was bundled in the large blanket, and between that and the pyjama pants she was almost completely covered.

When Doc was done, and it was stitched up neatly, he covered the spots he did. He slathered ointment onto the rest of her back, then that was covered as well. Preacher kissed the top of her head and leaned back slightly. Then he whipped his tee over his head and carefully pulled it down over hers. It was warm, and it smelled like him, so she decided she was never going it back.

"It's bigger than Snakes," she whispered, as Preacher pulled the blanket away and it fell to her knees.

"How would you know?" Snake asked curiously.

Macy shyly looked towards her brother. "I did your laundry for years. I stole one once to wear to bed."

"Fuck me," Snake said as he eyed her. "This relationship between me and you is going to change." Then he sat on the side of the tub and grabbed her hand. She looked at him in confusion.

"When mom died it broke something in me. She was the best, and her death has been something I've never been able to get over. She stopped her cancer treatments to have you. And I stupidly blamed you. Then not long after you were born, you got a bad cold. It turned into pneumonia and they hospitalized you. The doctors didn't think you'd make it, but you did. You were in the hospital more than once after that." Snake stopped and frowned at her.

"I lost mom. I didn't want to lose you too. Every time you went into the hospital I didn't think you'd come out. I figured if I shut down my feelings for you, then if you died, it wouldn't hurt so much." Snake shook his head and Macy could see the sadness he was dealing with.

"It was hard not showing you any love. You're my baby sister for god's sake. Then you show up with dad over this Pike shit, and you're basically thrown at me. I thought getting you a job at the laundromat would give you a bit of independence. I never in a million years thought you'd get hurt. That's on me," Snake huffed.

Macy squeezed his hand. "What are you saying?" she asked.

"I'm saying your my god damned little sister. A big brother's supposed to keep you safe. A big brother's supposed to make sure you know love. I didn't do either. I don't expect you to ever forgive me."

"I forgive you," she hurried to assure him.

"What?" Snake questioned as he blinked at her. "You can't just forget the way I've been treating you. It's not like I was an ass for a day or two, it's been your whole fucking life."

"I forgive you," she repeated a little louder.

Snake sighed, and she got frustrated. "I've loved you my whole life, no matter what. You're telling me things I've been waiting a long time to hear. I'm not wasting a minute making you feel bad and taking time to think about it. I need my big brother," she cried.

Snake moved quick then and pulled her gently against his chest. One hand went to her waist, and the other went to the back of her head.

"I don't deserve to have you as a sister," he growled. "But I promise I'll be the big brother you deserve from now on."

Snake pulled her back and studied her as he tilted his head. "Why Preacher? Of all the guys in the club, you picked the fucking president. What the hell are you thinking?"

"He called me Hummingbird," she whispered.

Her brother stared at her again. "That's it?" he said.

Macy blinked and tilted her head just like he had, and she heard Preacher growl behind her.

"He saw me," she admitted as she turned to Preacher. "He saw me, and he stayed."

"Jesus," Snake growled, but she wasn't done.

"And I really like my shower head," she finished, even though that part was for Preacher.

Then she smiled when Preacher threw back his head and laughed.

"Well how the fuck am I going to kick his ass now?" Snake growled.

Chapter Twenty Two
Preacher

Preacher carried a very sleepy Macy into the living room. Between the pain, the emotions, and the drugs, she was fading quickly. He had wrapped her in the blanket again, and he was trying to hold her gently without hurting her back.

"Jesus Snake," he complained when he stopped and the prospect almost slammed into his back. He had to admit he almost liked it better when Snake hated his sister, he knew now they weren't going to have a minute of privacy. The prospect was taking this making up for past mistakes shit seriously.

"Pack up what shit you want from this place, and everything your sister brought with her. If it doesn't fit on your bike call Smoke and have him bring a truck," Preacher ordered.

"You taking her to the clubhouse?" Snake questioned sharply.

"Well, I'm not fucking leaving her here," Preacher growled.

"Great, she can stay in my room," Snake declared, as he aimed a glare at him.

"Not happening," Preacher snarled. "But we can argue about that later. Right now I want her settled, then I want to fuck someone up."

Snake nodded, even though he still looked pissed, then he turned and headed to the bedroom. Dragon chuckled as he watched them go.

"Shadow's going to love this," Dragon smirked. "Let me guess, you'll get out of a beating because Snake's only a prospect."

"Fuck off," Preacher growled. Then he turned to Doc. "You mind riding my Harley back?"

"Sure thing," Doc replied with a chin lift. "Just don't use a seatbelt and turn her a bit so she rests on her side. That numbing medication I gave her won't last long. Once she's settled, I'll give her something else."

"Appreciated," Preacher responded.

Fifteen minutes later Preacher had his Hummingbird curled up in his bed and almost asleep. Doc had given her a heavy dose of pain meds and she was quietly watching him.

"Your going be okay Hummingbird?" Preacher asked, not hiding his concern in the least.

"I always am baby cakes," Macy whispered, then her eyes closed and didn't open. He chuckled, kissed her head, then backed away, sad that life had been so difficult for her. Quietly he headed out the door and made his way to the common room.

"I'm headed to the laundromat to have a little chat with the owners," Preacher announced to the room. "Anyone want to tag along?"

Heads turned and chairs scraped back, and he was happy to see Dragon, Steele, Dagger, Wrench, Navaho and Tripp headed his way. When he heard the main door shut, he looked that way and just caught the prospect patch on Snake's back before it slammed shut.

"Shit," Preacher muttered with a shake of his head. "We better move before Snake gets a wild hair and kills everyone."

As they headed to their bikes, Preacher was surprised to see Snake's bike still there, and Snake nowhere to be found. He pulled out his phone and hit the brothers name.

"Where the fuck are you?" Preacher demanded.

"I'm picking something up, I'll meet you there," Snake growled into the phone.

"Fine," Preacher sighed then disconnected.

"I'm packing toys," Dagger announced as he sauntered up beside him. "I saw your girl. I figure it's warranted."

"Trike's not coming?" Preacher asked with a raised brow.

"Nah, he won't leave his baby momma," Dagger grumbled.

Preacher nodded and made another call.

"Preacher," Darren answered on the first ring. "I'm hoping you got some action for me, it's getting damn quiet around here," he complained.

"Fucking cops," Preacher growled. Then he shook his head when Darren chuckled.

"I'm giving you the heads up that we're heading to the laundromat to have a chat with the owners, and it won't be a friendly chat," Preacher informed him.

"Shit," Darren grunted. "Care to elaborate on why?"

"I claimed Snake's sister. She worked there. Somehow today she burned her entire back on a hot roller. Said the owner came at her yelling and carrying a long metal ruler," Preacher explained.

"I'll give you a fifteen minute head start, then me and Colin will meet you there. We'll run interference and keep things quiet," Darren immediately told him.

"Dagger's coming," Preacher added. "Don't know how quiet this will be."

"Well then Colin will get broken in quickly," Darren chuckled.

"Yeah," Preacher sighed before he hung up.

"Mount up," he yelled as he climbed on his hog and started it up. He nodded at Steele, who was at his side, then twisted the throttle and headed out the gate. It was time to get a little frustration out.

Chapter Twenty Three
Preacher

Preacher pulled up to the laundromat and shut down his bike. He waited as his brothers did the same. When they were all off and by his side he prowled towards the entrance. He almost had his hand on the handle when a car pulling into the lot caught his attention. He wasn't surprised when Darren and Colin stepped out.

"I thought I had a twenty-minute head start?" Preacher growled in annoyance.

"You did. It's not our fault you took almost that long to get here," Darren answered with a grin.

Preacher was going to respond when another Harley came barrelling into the parking lot. He threw up his hands when a brother climbed off.

"Lucifer, why am I not surprised?" he asked.

"If Colin's here it means he's not chasing my woman," Lucifer happily replied. "Plus, I'm new, I've missed a lot of the action."

"Hey," Colin complained. "I'm not chasing your woman anymore."

Lucifer threw up his hands. "Because I'm always with her dumb ass."

"Jesus," Preacher growled. "You two duke it out, I'm headed in." Then he yanked the handle and went inside. He wasn't surprised when everyone of the fuckers followed him inside.

"You want leather cleaned, extra ten dollars," a small Chinese woman yelled as she eyed their vests.

"Not why we're here," Preacher sneered. "You came at my girl with a ruler. She burned her back because of you."

"Ah, you useless Macy's guy. You can do better than her. She terrible employee. I her boss, Mrs. Tang."

"Useless Macy?" Preacher growled as he took a menacing step forward.

"She never get work done, she slow, she always late," Mrs. Tang complained.

"Excuse me," Wrench said a little too politely. "You go by these clocks?" he asked as he pointed to the wall.

"Yes," Mrs. Tang confirmed. "Very reliable."

"Your clocks ten fucking minutes fast," Wrench told her.

"So you fucked her around, then you hurt her," Preacher roared. All the bikers stepped forward as a group to back him up. Colin and Darren smirked as they leaned against the counter and watched the back and forth.

"I no hurt her. She stupid. She back into steamer," Mrs. Tang yelled. "You get out of my shop. You here to cause trouble."

"You've got an awfully big laundromat for such a small town," Tripp declared as he eyed the back. "I'm surprised the farmers around here bring their work clothes to you."

Preacher watched as Tripp stepped forward and started going through the racks of clean clothes.

Darren slapped Colin on the back. "You can take a cop and turn him into a biker, but he's still going to be a cop." Then he chuckled as Tripp aimed a middle finger at his old partner.

"This is a small town. Not a lot of well off people in it. Why the hell are most of the clothes suits and cocktail dresses?" Tripp demanded.

Mrs. Tang shifted on her feet and glared at Tripp. "My brother own big laundromat in the city. He send me clothes, I clean, I send back."

Then they blinked in surprise as she produced a baseball bat from behind the counter and slammed Tripp on the shoulder with it. He roared in pain, then turned and ripped the bat from her hands.

"That's assault," Darren announced helpfully.

Before Darren could say more Preacher headed for the back.

"You no go back there. Stupid girl broke steamer," she yelled as she followed him. "You get out."

Preacher stared at the steamer, and all he could focus on was the small spot of blood that was on one of the rollers. Then he saw the large metal ruler laying on the ground.

His brothers surrounded Mrs. Tang and blocked the only way out. Preacher picked up the heavy ruler and held it out towards the Chinese lady.

"Is this what you went after my girl with?" he growled furiously.

Then all hell broke loose, as something massive crashed into the front of the building. Glass broke, ceiling tiles fell, and bricks rained down.

Preacher peered through the dust, stunned to see Snake sitting in the bulldozer's cab they stored at the compound. The entire bulldozer was now in the store's front where they had stood only a minute ago.

"You thought you could fuck with my sister," Snake bellowed at a horrified Mrs. Tang. "I don't think so."

"You sure you still want to be a cop in this town," Darren chuckled at a pale looking Colin. "These bikers do things a little differently."

Chapter Twenty Four
Preacher

Preacher glared at Dagger as he saw the brothers face light up.

"Finally, someone I can relate too. Brother, you're my new partner in crime," Dagger yelled at Snake with a massive grin.

Snake ignored him, and Preacher watched in silence as he jumped down from the tractor. He dusted himself off and stomped towards Mrs. Tang.

"You knew Macy was my sister, why would you fuck with her?" Snake growled.

"I not know. How I know?" Mrs. Tang denied. "I thought you sleeping with useless Macy?"

"Stop fucking calling her useless Macy?" Preacher snarled as he joined the conversation.

"You destroy business. You owe me money," she stupidly yelled.

"Dagger," Preacher called, done with her completely. "You bring any dynamite?"

"Does a bear shit in the woods?" Dagger responded with a shake of his head.

"You can't just blow up a business?" Colin argued as he stepped towards them.

"No, no, no," Mrs. Tang yelled as she picked up bars of soap and threw them at Dagger.

"That's assault," Darren once again helpfully advised them.

Preacher ignored them all and turned back to Dagger. He snickered when he saw Dagger had picked up a garbage can lid, and the soap was bouncing harmlessly off it.

"You want total annihilation or you got something specific in mind?" Dagger asked as soap pelted the lid.

"I want those fucking steamers taken out," Preacher growled. "My girls blood has stained one. Blow the fucking things to bits."

Dagger nodded, put down the lid, and pulled a stick of dynamite out of his pocket. He immediately wedged it between the steamers. Once it was secure, he pulled out a lighter and lit the end.

"I'm pretty accurate, but you still may want to take cover," he warned, as he headed back and ducked down behind the tractor.

All the brothers did the same except for Colin, who stood staring at the dynamite like he was in a trance. Wrench walked over to him, grabbed him by the back of his shirt, and hauled him over to the tractor.

"You can't just blow up the steamers," Colin mumbled. "This can't be legal."

"Rat," Lucifer yelled, gaining Colin's attention.

"What?" Colin questioned looking confused.

"Big fucking rat," Lucifer snarled.

Then the dynamite blew, and once again dust, ceiling tiles, and bricks rained down on them.

"Jesus," Dagger yelled. "Anyone know of a good dry cleaner. It's a bugger getting these vests cleaned."

Everyone chuckled except for Colin, who was glaring at Lucifer. "There was no rat," he angrily shouted.

Preacher shook his head as Lucifer just smirked. Then they all stopped and stared, as a shit ton of one hundred dollar bills started to rain down around them.

"Looks like good old Mrs. Tang is using the laundromat to front a money laundering business," Tripp chuckled. "Now that explains the suits and cocktail dresses. I bet the money goes in and out that way."

"My money," Mrs. Tang yelled. "You leave my money alone." Then the crazy lady started running around trying to scoop it all up.

"You taking her in?" Preacher asked Darren. "Or can we blow her up too?"

Colin started sputtering at that. "Are you fucking serious?" he choked.

"She hurt my girl," Preacher snarled. "She's getting off fucking lucky."

Darren walked forward then with a pair of handcuffs. After getting kicked in the shin twice, he hobbled off with Mrs. Tang in tow.

"You're under arrest for money laundering," Darren explained to her as she struggled with him.

"And assault," Tripp yelled.

"Don't fucking blow the building," Colin hollered on his way out. "I need what's left for evidence." As Dagger started to bend, Colin added, "the money's evidence too."

"All of it?" Dagger pouted as he stood. "You're no fun anymore."

"You satisfied?" Navaho asked as he silently approached.

"Guess it's the best I can hope for," Preacher sighed. "I have a feeling she'll be locked up for a while." Then he turned to Snake. "Pull that god damned thing out of the building and drive it back."

"Right," Snake easily agreed. Then the brothers followed him out the side of the building, where a wall used to be.

After they climbed on their Harley's, they stopped to watch Snake. The prospect started up the tractor, and Preacher watched as the scoop suddenly lifted. As he backed out the scoop tore the ceiling down, and the whole front of the building, apartment and all, caved in. Once he was clear, he didn't look back, just turned onto the road and headed home.

Preacher could do nothing but throw back his head and laugh.

Chapter Twenty Five
Macy

Macy woke slowly. Her back was throbbing, but she was relieved to see she had fallen asleep on her stomach. She opened her eyes and peered around the room. This room was different, and she knew right away she wasn't in Preacher's room anymore. The room didn't smell like his, and walls weren't painted a dark colour like Preacher's.

Macy panicked and tried to sit up, but it pulled at her back. She moaned painfully as she lied back down.

"Hey," she heard come from the corner of the room. "You need to be careful, honey."

Macy peered in the direction of the voice and saw a man sitting in a chair. It looked like he'd been fiddling with his phone. She would have worried, but he was wearing the same vest as the rest of the bikers.

"Preacher?" she asked quietly.

The biker smiled then. "Preacher left to take care of something. Doc was sitting with you, but he got called to the hospital. I'm Smoke," the biker informed her.

"Who's room am I in?" Macy questioned, then watched as the biker frown.

"Snake left with Preacher, but before he did, he carried you to his room. I tried to stop him but he was pretty determined. He's put me in a difficult spot," Smoke sighed. "If I leave you here, Preacher will get mad cause you're not where he left you. But if I carry you back, he'll get mad because I touched you. I'm in trouble no matter what I do."

"You won't get in trouble," she told the prospect. "I won't let you."

Smoke grinned at her. "You can't stop it."

"I can," Macy said, then changed the subject. "Smoke?" she questioned in reference to his odd name, then watched as his grin fell.

"I was trapped in a fire with Mario's woman. Someone had stabbed me in the leg a couple times and it wasn't looking good. His girl dislocated a shoulder trying to drag me out. It's not something I'm proud of," he sighed.

"Why?" she asked curiously.

"She had to save me, that's not how it should have happened," Smoke grumbled.

"So you were hurt, and she ran into a fire and tried to drag you out?" Macy questioned, not understanding.

"No," Smoke chuckled. "A stalker was after her. And a girl was murdered. I was being set up for it. The stalker grabbed me and tied me up, then grabbed her and tied her up too. Then they set the building we were in on fire," he explained.

"So she got untied and saved you?" she asked.

"No," he chuckled again. "I got untied and was untying her when the stalker came at me. She shot the stalker then tried to drag me out."

"Ah," Macy smiled, now understanding. "So you got free and helped her first. You saved the day.

You both would have been dead if you hadn't gotten free."

He tilted his head as he thought about what she said. A minute later he grinned at her. "I like you," Smoke admitted.

"So the name Smoke came from the fire?" she asked.

"Right," he said.

Then they heard Preacher bellowing her name.

"Here we go," Smoke complained, as he stood and shuffled closer to the bed. "It was nice knowing you," he commented sadly.

Macy frowned at the poor biker, then watched as Preacher stomped into the room. He took one look at her and sagged with relief. Then turned furious eyes on the prospect.

"Why the hell is she in Snake's room?" Preacher roared.

"Ummmm," was all Smoke got out before he was slammed up against the wall.

"Preacher," Macy whispered softly, then watched as his eyes snapped to hers. "I was asleep when Snake carried me here. I only just woke up. Smoke knew you wouldn't like it if he picked me up, so he left me here. I was just about to try to get up so I could go back to your room, but he begged me to wait for you. He didn't want me to hurt myself. It was actually really sweet of him."

Preacher turned his eyes to Smoke, sighed and let the biker go. "Okay," he huffed. "Smart thinking."

Macy winked at the prospect when he looked her way. He shot her a grin, then smartly fled the room.

Snake was standing in the doorway when it was clear. "She's my sister, she stays with me," he growled.

"She's my one, she belongs with me," Preacher countered.

They glared at each other and Macy started to get worried. "No fighting in front of me," she whispered. Then she watched in absolute surprise, as Preacher nodded, grabbed her brother by the back of his vest, and hauled him from the room.

Chapter Twenty Six
Preacher

Preacher dragged Snake down the hall. The prospect stumbled once, but caught himself as he tried to keep up. Snake struggled as he pulled at Preacher's fist, trying to dislodge him and not fall flat on his face at the same time. Preacher understood Snake was the one thing standing between him and his Hummingbird, so he wasn't budging. This was fucking ending now.

When Preacher passed Shadow in the hall, he bellowed an order at the brother. "Macy is in Snake's room. Help her to the common room now."

When Preacher reached the common room, he was happy to see almost all the brothers there. Of course, they had just gotten back from the laundromat, and gossip was running rampant.

He shoved Snake against the bar and growled "don't fucking move." The prospect took one step forward, and when Preacher raised his eyebrow, he stopped and crossed his arms over his massive chest. Snake angrily leaned back against the bar and glared instead, which Preacher ignored.

A minute later the bar had quieted, as everyone noticed something was about to go down. Shadow sauntered in with Macy in his arms and headed straight for him. Preacher gently took her from the brother and kissed her head.

"You okay Hummingbird?" he asked. She looked a little unsure, but gave him an honest answer.

"A bit sore, and kind of scared right now," Macy softly informed him as she glanced at all the bikers spread out around the room.

"Nothing to be afraid of," Preacher assured her. "Bikers need to hash things out. Usually we do it publicly, that way there's no fucking playground antics. Me and your brother need to get a few things straight, and we're doing that now."

Macy glanced uncertainly at her brother. He straightened from the bar and smirked at her.

"Ummm, okay," she whispered as she bit her lip.

"That's my girl," Preacher grinned. Then he kissed her head and placed her directly on the bar so she was sitting upright and her feet were hanging off.

"You couldn't find a chair?" she asked quietly, as she blinked and tilted her head.

"Jesus," Preacher cursed. Then he moved close, grabbed her behind the neck, and slammed his lips down on hers. He only kissed her a minute before he pulled back and glanced around the room. Snake looked ready to throttle him, but the rest of the brothers looked stunned.

Then Dagger went and dove under a table, and all eyes turned to him.

"What the fuck are you doing?" Dragon growled. Dagger poked his head out and glared at the brother.

"I'm not standing out there in the open. Preacher once said god would strike him down with lightning before he ever took a woman," the biker reminded them. "I don't want to be in the line of fire."

Preacher threw up his arms in agitation. "That was ages ago," he growled.

"That was two weeks ago," Dagger shot back.

"Well that was before I met my Hummingbird," he sneered.

Then Preacher watched as all the bikers collectively "awww'd".

"Fucking bikers," he complained. Then he turned to Snake.

"You got a problem with me claiming your sister?" he asked.

"I definitely got a problem with you claiming my sister," Snake grunted.

"You ain't been much of a brother to her. Why the fuck should you care?" Preacher questioned.

"I'm making up for lost time," Snake told him angrily.

"Five hits is what I got for claiming your sister," Shadow yelled helpfully. "I want to see Snake get the same thing."

Steele held up his hands then to calm the bikers as they all started shouting. "Rules only apply to patched members. Snake isn't patched in yet, so technically there's nothing he can do."

"I can still punch him," Snake argued. "I'm her god damned brother."

"You can," Steele agreed. "But he's the president, and you'd be thrown out regardless of your reasons. You want to be a biker, I suggest you don't go that route."

"So I just sit back and watch as he claims her, with no say at all," Snake growled. "That's fucking insane. And what happens if I'm not not patched in?" he bellowed. "I'm kicked out of the club and I'll never fucking see her again. I'm trying to repair this relationship, and you all are trying to destroy it," he yelled as he slammed his fist down on the bar.

Preacher smirked. They'd pushed Snake far, and the ass had finally said the one thing Preacher and the brothers were waiting to hear.

Chapter Twenty Seven
Macy

Macy didn't know what was going down. She watched as Preacher and her brother glared at each other. Snake's change in attitude still floored her, but he seemed to be serious about it. He was turning into the brother she'd always wanted.

Snake was shouting and threatening to beat Preacher up, and she was getting concerned. If she understood right, Preacher wasn't supposed to date her, and she didn't like the sound of that at all.

"Wait," Macy quietly interrupted. She didn't think anyone heard her, but of course Preacher did. He turned to her immediately.

"Hummingbird?" he questioned with a raised brow.

"I don't understand," Macy said as she rubbed at her head. "Are they saying we can't see each other?" she asked sadly.

Preacher growled at her, then moved to stand between her legs. His hand immediately caressed her cheek, and she leaned into the touch.

"No one is stopping me from claiming you, and I'm claiming you not dating you, there's a big difference. The problem is that we have a club rule that no one can get involved with a patched in brother's sibling. If it happens, the patched member gets five hits to the brother breaking the rule, and gets to approve the relationship or not. It's the biker way," he gently explained.

"But my brother isn't patched in yet?" she whispered, knowing the difference.

"Exactly," Snake sneered. "So apparently what the club is saying, is that my opinion means nothing. Even though I'm your brother, I have no rights."

Macy looked at Preacher sadly. "I'm falling for you but I don't like that. I love my brother, and I think his opinion counts."

Preacher sighed. "Then I guess we better patch him in and do this right," he decided.

Her eyes flew up to latch onto his. "Your patching him in?" she asked in surprise.

"You want your brothers opinion to count and that's the only way it will. Plus the fuckers saying some things that we've been waiting to hear from him. You don't treat family the way he has, and because of that, we didn't want to make him a part of ours. But he's redeeming himself, and he's turning into a man we'd be happy to accept into the Knight's," Preacher told her.

"Thank you," Macy sincerely said.

"Don't thank me, only a true biker would drive a tractor through the front of Mrs. Tang's laundromat," he chuckled.

"What?" Macy asked as her eyes flew to her brother. He looked extremely uncomfortable now.

"A few of us went to have a little chat with your boss. Your brother drove a tractor through the front and we blew up the steamers. Mrs. Tang also went to jail for money laundering," Preacher imparted.

Macy blinked and tilted her head, and Preacher growled.

"Steele bring the fucking vest so we can get this shit over with and I can claim my fucking girl," he growled.

A minute later, she watched as Steele pulled a new leather vest from a box and handed it to Preacher. Preacher then motioned for her brother to head over. He did so without question.

"Snake, I had my fucking doubts about you, and honestly we were ready to cut you lose. But you've done an about face and we couldn't be fucking prouder. You've proven to us that family is important to you, and that's what this whole club is about," he explained.

Then Macy watched as Preacher held out his hand for the prospect vest and replaced it with the new one. Once it was on, Preacher yelled, "welcome to the fucking Knight's brother."

She smiled when cheers went up and they surrounded her brother. She was happy for him, and he looked like he had everything he wanted. When the cheering died down Preacher raised his hands for silence.

"Now you're a patched in member, the rule applies. I may be the president, but that doesn't mean I'm a fucking pansy. I'll take my hits and I'll do it standing proud," he announced.

"What?" Macy asked in horror.

"You're going to be my girl, you need to get used to how bikers do things Hummingbird. I'm claiming you, and I'm doing it right. I can take a couple hits if it means I get to spend my life with you," Preacher told her.

A tear ran down Macy's face as she turned to her brother. He nodded at her, and she turned back to Preacher.

"Okay," she whispered. "But I don't want to watch."

Preacher kissed her soundly, then turned to Snake and motioned to the door. She was shocked when all the brothers but Doc and Navaho left.

"Jesus Shadow," Preacher bellowed as he walked out. "You don't have to be so fucking excited about this." The brother was in the goddamned lead.

"Come on honey," Navaho soothed. "I'll get you some food while Doc checks your back."

Chapter Twenty Eight
Preacher

Preacher stepped outside, followed by Snake and pretty much the entire club. He was happy to see that Doc and Navaho stayed inside to look after his girl. She didn't need to see this. She was claimed by him though, so with him being the president, she'd have to get use to this shit. He turned to Steele as he thought of something.

"Do me a favour and call your woman. Get her and the others to the common room. Macy needs to meet them, plus I figure they can help explain this to her," he ordered. "I'm pretty sure they're all holed up at Trike's waiting for Misty to go into labour,"

"Right," his VP agreed. "Just don't fucking start until I finish the call."

Preacher glared at him. "The call will take seconds, you'll be fine." Then he turned to address the brothers.

"Make a fucking circle around us, and give us some room," he bellowed. He watched as Dagger came out with some paper. "You rate his fucking punches, and I'm going after you when this is done."

"No worries," Dagger said. "You'll be in no shape to do me much damage." Preacher could only growl at the ass. He was probably right.

Dragon interpreted. "As sergeant of arms I'll make sure he's taken care of," he claimed as he smirked at Dagger.

Dagger turned a glare at Dragon. "So you fight his battles for him now."

Preacher chuckled. "No, he defends the club when they need it."

"It's kind of his job dumb ass," Steele added as he ended his call.

"Hmmmm," Dagger huffed as he dropped his papers. Preacher ignored him and turned to Snake.

"You're a patched in member now. Usually this wouldn't happen because you were a prospect when I claimed her. But I've gone through this with my sister, and I understand your pain. You'll get five hits, no more. There are no other rules except no rings and no groin shots. Understood," Preacher asked.

"Understood," Snake replied with a smirk.

"No filming," Preacher bellowed at Dagger. The ass jumped and almost dropped his phone, but he did put it away.

Preacher took off his cut and handed it to Steele, then nodded at Snake that he was ready. The first hit caught him in the mouth so fast he wasn't ready. He rocked back a foot, but thankfully didn't go down. He felt his lip split though, and it pissed him off. He spit out blood, then readied himself for the next hit.

Preacher wasn't surprised when the second hit caught him in the stomach. He swallowed the pain and was thankful he hadn't cracked anything. Of course that was fucking stupid, because the second hit was in the same spot. Preacher immediately felt the snap and knew a rib was either cracked or broken.

"Three hits down, two more to go," Shadow yelled helpfully. The fucker was enjoying this way too much.

The third hit caught Preacher in the shoulder, and he rocked slightly on his feet. The last hit caught him under the eye, and he knew it wasn't going to take long before it was swelled up.

"You fucking promise me your going to treat my sister better than I did," Snake ordered as he shook out his first. Preacher was happy to see Snake's knuckles were slightly swollen and torn.

"I give you my word," Preacher vowed. "That girl will know nothing but love. I'll protect her with my fucking life."

Snake nodded. "Then you have my blessing. Treat her as you say and we'll be good."

Preacher nodded. "But I expect the same of you. You've treated her like shit," he complained. He raised his hand when Snake would have argued. "I understand and see you've changed, but I expect you to protect her and show her kindness from here out."

Snake immediately nodded. Preacher held out his hand and his new brother took it. When they shook though, Preacher may have squeezed just a little harder than necessary on his bruised knuckles. The brother grimaced but otherwise held his ground.

Preacher was more than happy with his decision to patch Snake in. The brother was already proving himself.

"Let's head in and have a fucking drink," Preacher ordered. "Once the pain sets in more I'm not going to want to feel it."

The brothers chuckled, but he wasn't surprised to hear them all following behind him.

Chapter Twenty Nine
Macy

Macy sat on the stool eating the sandwich that Navaho made her as Doc checked her back. She was wearing Preacher's shirt, and it was easy for him to lift up the back without exposing her front. It was so large it almost hit her knees. When he touched a particularly tender spot, she cried out.

"You hurting our newest girl Doc?" came a girl's voice from down the hall. Macy turned her head and was surprised to see seven girls headed her way.

"Just checking her stitches Cassie," Doc explained with a welcoming smile. "Her back was burned, kind of like November's legs and Alexandria's hands. She'll be okay, but it will take a bit."

"Sandwiches all around?" Navaho asked as the girls spread out down the bar. There was one extremely pregnant girl, and the rest were laughing as she struggled to get on a stool.

"How about if we put you on the couch? I can drag a table over and some chairs. I think you'd be more comfortable," Navaho chuckled.

The girl looked at him in relief. "I'd really appreciate that," she sighed.

"Come on Macy," Cassie smiled, as she grabbed her plate with her unfinished sandwich and walked away. Macy watched her a minute then jumped down and followed. She really wanted her sandwich back, and it seemed Doc was finished with her.

Navaho got them all situated then left, presumably to make more sandwiches.

"I'm Cassie," the girl who took her sandwich said, which she already knew. Then she pointed to each girl in turn. "The pregnant girl is Misty, the hippy is Fable, the one with the baby is Ali, the baby is Catherine, that's November, that's Alexandria, and the last girl is Tiffany."

"Wow," Macy grinned. "There's a lot of you."

"But I'm the most important," Tiffany declared. Macy blinked at her.

"Um, okay," she replied in confusion.

"I'm your sister," Tiffany announced. "Or at least I will be when you and my brother tie the knot."

"Your Preacher's sister," Macy said in surprise.

Tiffany frowned. "Has he told you anything?" she asked.

"I know there's biker business that I can't interfere with," Macy answered.

"Oh we always interfere," November chuckled. "They try to keep us out of it but it usually backfires on them."

"So who are you all married to?" Macy questioned, quickly changing the subject.

"I'm married to Jaxon," Ali piped up. When Macy looked confused again, Ali filled her in. "Dragon, but we were together before he got that name, so I use the one I'm used to."

"I'm married to Trike, or Brody," Misty told her.

"I'm married to Mario," Alexandria piped up. "He's kind of an honorary member. We live up on the hill. He doesn't wear a vest, and he tries to keep his business separate. Oh, and he drives an Aston Martin instead of a motorcycle."

"His business?" Macy questioned with a frown.

"Yeah," Alexandria sighed. "I can't really talk about that. A lot of its illegal." Before she could question that, November spoke up.

"I'm married to Jude. The club calls him Lucifer now, but I call him Lucy," she explained. "It really pisses him off," she said with a huge grin.

"I'm married to Steele," Cassie said. "His real names Ryker.

"I'm married to Tripp," Fable grinned.

"And I'm married to Shadow," Tiffany explained. "He doesn't really tell anybody his real name, so I'm not sure if I should."

"Hey," November said. "They gossip worse than we do. You can tell us, no one will know."

Tiffany looked around to make sure Navaho and Doc were out of hearing distance. "His names Tyson."

"Really?" Misty smiled. "That's not bad."

"It's weird," Fable declared. "It doesn't really suit him."

"True enough," Misty agreed, then she gasped. Ali who had been sitting on the couch beside her with the baby, jumped up.

"I get peed on enough by Catherine. I don't need you peeing on me too," Ali complained.

Misty just stared at her friend. "I didn't pee," she huffed.

"Oh my god," Fable cried. "Your water broke."

"Time to go to the hospital," Cassie ordered. "We can load up in two trucks."

"What about the guys?" Macy asked as she eyed two men with them.

"Jesus," November complained. "It's going to be a shit show if they come." The other girls nodded their heads in complete agreement.

"Can I at least come?" Doc asked from his seat at the bar.

Misty smiled then. "That would be appreciated," she said. Then November turned to Navaho with a grin.

"Ten minute head start?" November asked with a raised brow, and Macy watched as the beautiful man threw back his head and laughed.

Chapter Thirty
Preacher

Preacher walked into the clubhouse slowly. He was fucking hurting. Snake was one tough fucker, and he wasn't expecting to feel this bad afterwards. He almost wished he'd stuck to the rules, but Preacher had earned the respect of the club, and had worked fucking hard to get it. He kept that respect by doing stupid shit like what he just did.

Preacher stepped inside and headed for the bar. Navaho was there, and immediately Smoke headed around to help him. He was surprised when Trike sat down beside him.

"Thought you weren't straying from your girl's side?" Preacher questioned.

"Sniper called and told me the fight was about to start. I didn't want to miss it," Trike grinned. "Plus, I brought Misty up here to hang with the girls."

Preacher sat up straight and looked around the bar. The girls weren't there now though. He frowned when he caught Navaho looking at his watch. Suddenly there was a beeping noise coming from it.

"What the fucks with your watch?" Preacher asked. "And where the hell are the girls?"

Navaho grinned and looked to Trike. He grinned bigger when Lucifer joined them.

"Klutz told me to give them a ten minute head start," Navaho grinned. Preacher's back immediately went straight.

"A ten minute head start where?" he growled.

"Misty's water broke, and they took her to the hospital," Navaho explained.

"What the fuck?" Trike roared as he jumped off the stool. He was stopped immediately when Navaho reached over the bar and grabbed his shoulder. The biker easy held a panicked Trike in place.

"One," Navaho said. "Your girls in labour and fucking huge, she's not moving quickly. Two, the truck and SUV are parked further away from the bikes. And three, you know those girls will fight for a couple minutes about who goes in what vehicle and who sits where. And four, Doc went with them."

"So," Trike yelled in agitation as he pulled at Navaho's hand.

"He fucking means they're probably just pulling out of the parking lot dumb ass," Lucifer interrupted.

Trike turned to glare at him. "It was your girl that asked for the ten minute head start. She's a nut."

Preacher sighed and stepped between the brothers before they started wrestling. "You want to head out, or wait until they make it to the hospital and she has the baby without you?"

Trike blinked and then turned angry eyes on him. "She isn't having that fucking baby without me."

"Right," Preacher snorted. "Then get on the back of Sniper's bike, so when we catch them you can jump in the vehicle with her."

"And shimmy back," Sniper yelled as they made their way out the door. "I don't want any of your body parts touching my body parts."

Preacher chuckled as he climbed on his Harley and started it up. He could actually use Doc too after the hits he took from Snake, so maybe it was good they were headed to the hospital. He pulled out of the gate with all the bikers following him, and then outright laughed when he saw the two vehicles not too far down the road.

Seconds later they had the vehicles surrounded. He caught Doc's eye and motioned for him to stop. The man nodded and stopped right in the middle of the road. As soon as he did, Trike jumped off Sniper's Harley, and ripped open the passenger door where Misty was sitting.

"You left without telling me," Trike yelled at his clearly miserable wife.

"It was November's idea," Misty sniffed.

"Hey," November yelled. "Don't throw me under the bus, you all agreed."

"So you were going to the hospital without me? Do you remember what happened the last time?" Trike yelled. "You were kidnaped, shot, and buried alive in a fucking mine. Do not think you're going to the hospital without me."

With Trike done, Misty broke into hysterical sobs. He threw up his arms in agitation, then climbed into the vehicle awkwardly and somehow managed to get her so she sat in his lap. Preacher eyed Macy who was in the backseat.

"Want to ride with me Hummingbird?" he questioned.

She didn't answer, just grinned and proceeded to climb over November and get out. Preacher chuckled at the look of surprise on Klutz' face.

"I could have moved," November grumbled.

But Preacher ignored her, as his girl hurried over, kissed his battered cheek, and took the helmet from him.

"You okay?" Macy whispered as she eyed his bloody face.

"Hop on, and I'll be perfect," Preacher grinned. And he was, cause that's just what his girl did.

Chapter Thirty One
Macy

Macy sat in the waiting room of the hospital, curled up against Preacher. All the bikers had shown, and they packed the waiting room. A nurse had seen Preacher and he now had an ice pack on his cheek, ointment on his lip, and his cracked ribs were wrapped. Of course she knew all this because he had dragged her into the exam room with him. Apparently bad things happened at the hospital and Preacher wasn't letting her out of his sight.

It was a four hour wait until they finally got news, and Macy spent all of it glaring at her brother. She understood why Snake had done it, and she appreciated him defending her, but she didn't like the injuries Preacher had suffered. Although, she had to give Preacher credit, he was sitting there acting like he wasn't in pain.

Finally Doc came back and announced that Trike and Misty had their little boy. The baby was perfect, and he explained Trike would be out in about fifteen minutes to show him off. That wasn't really allowed, but apparently Doc didn't care and not one of the staff moved to argue with him.

When Trike came out, he was wearing hospital scrubs and a grin so big Macy was amazed it fit his face. It was obvious he was very proud to be a dad. When the girls jumped up and rushed him they dragged Macy with them. She peered down at the baby as they were busy shouting congratulations, and couldn't help falling instantly fell in love.

"Now you're all going to have your women demanding you knock them up," Dagger laughed. "We're going to have to build a fucking daycare." When all the brothers glared at him, he only laughed harder.

"Well I'm already pregnant," Cassie declared with a grin, "so my man doesn't have to worry about that."

Steele's eyes just about bugged out of his head. "Your fucking pregnant?" he stated, as his eyes shot to her flat stomach. Macy watched as Cassie smiled at the huge biker.

"Six weeks," Cassie declared proudly.

Steele was across the room in seconds and had her up in his arms. "Excuse us," he said to the room in general as he carried her away.

"You can't get her pregnant again dumb ass, she already is," Dagger hollered after them, but once again he was ignored.

"What did you name him?" Tiffany asked as she grinned at the tiny baby boy.

"Brady," Trike told her. "Misty said it was the closest she could get to my real name."

"Hmmm," Ali sighed wistfully. "Brody and Brady. I like it."

"I have to take him back," Trike told them after a minute. "I don't want to get Doc in trouble for being out here with him." Then he turned to Sniper. "Your sister's asking for you. You can come back with me. And Doc said to give us about twenty minutes, then the rest of you can come back too."

Trike said his goodbyes and headed back with Sniper hot on his heels, so Macy made her way back to Preacher.

"You care to wait another twenty minutes, or you want out of here?" Preacher asked her as he brushed her hair back off her face.

"I can wait," Macy assured him. "I don't mind."

Preacher held her close being careful of her back, and when it was time, they all headed back. The room was packed with all the bikers and their women but nobody cared. Misty accepted the hugs and well wishes and seemed to thrive on the attention. The baby was passed around, and even Macy was allowed to hold him.

"You want a baby of your own?" Preacher whispered in her ear as he moved closer. She shivered as she turned to look up at him.

"I want a family of my own. I want to show a baby the love I never got. I want something that's all mine," Macy quietly replied.

"I guess we're going to have to move this relationship along a little faster than," he growled. "Because I'd like to be the one to give you all that."

Macy smiled up at him in awe. "I'm falling for you Preacher," she told him.

"Well I'm already there, so hurry the fuck up and catch up," he ordered sharply.

She blinked and tilted her head, and the next thing she knew Preacher was growling and yanking the baby out of her arms to hand off to someone else. Then she was pulled tight against his chest and he was kissing her.

"Anyone else going to make a baby today?" Dagger smirked.

Then Dagger said no more, as Snake hauled back his fist and caught Dagger right in the jaw. The biker blinked once then fell back against the wall. The bikers all stood there in surprised shock until Dragon spoke up.

"Well it had to happen eventually," he declared, and the room erupted in laughter.

Chapter Thirty Two
Preacher

Preacher loved being at the hospital, but he wanted to get back to the clubhouse with Macy. Plus, he was worried about his room. He didn't want to be gone long enough for anyone to have a chance to "decorate" it. He'd seen the other rooms, and it definitely wasn't for him.

Preacher pulled up next to the clubhouse and held out his hand to help his girl off. She immediately placed her tiny hand in his and let him assist her. When he had her helmet put away he frowned, seeing the intense way she was studying him.

"Why the look?" he questioned curiously.

"Snake got some good hits in," Macy pouted. "I'm worried about you." He leaned down and placed his lips against hers, giving her a soft, but long kiss. When he pulled back, he smiled at her dazed expression.

"I'm okay Hummingbird, and from now on every time you ask me, I'm going to ask you about your back," he vowed.

Macy nodded at him. "I won't ask you again," she promised.

"Good, But I'm still going to ask you," Preacher warned her. Then he took her hand and led her into the clubhouse before she could reply.

Preacher ignored the bikers who had beat him back and were lounging in the common area. He wanted to talk to Macy and figure some things out. He reached his room and threw open the door, fully expecting glitter to float out. Thankfully nothing happened, and he was happy to see it looked exactly the same as he'd left it. He pulled her inside and shut the door with a relieved sigh.

"Are you serious about being mine and starting a family with me?" Preacher questioned. He'd claimed her already, but he wanted to make sure they were on the same page.

When Macy nodded, he led her over to the window. His room was at the back of the clubhouse and he had a clear view of the lake. Preacher positioned her in front of him, then leaned into her back gently and wrapped her in his arms. He pointed in the distance and smiled when she followed his finger. He heard her sharp intake of breath and knew she saw the cabins and the lake.

"That's amazing," Macy whispered. "What are the cabins used for?"

"When a biker finds his one, he wants privacy," Preacher explained. "It's not possible to have a wife and kid stay in their room, and it's not practical. I let them build small cabins by the lake. It's good for them, and it's good for the club because it keeps them close."

"So you're showing me because?" she prompted.

"You want a life with me, but I don't want you to expect a cabin too. I'm sure the girls will jump all over explaining how that's what all the guys do, but I want you to realize I'm not one of the guys. As the president of The Stone Knight's, I need to be where everyone has access to me."

Macy turned in his arms and tilted her head back so she could look up at him. "So you don't want a cabin?" she asked. "Are we staying in your room?"

"Do you trust me?" Preacher pushed. He smiled when she nodded quickly. "There's something I want to show you." He then took her hand again, left the room, and headed up the back staircase. When they reached the top, he opened the door and hit the lights.

"This is the second floor loft," Preacher explained as he stepped inside. "It's not used anymore. There's two massive rooms and a full bathroom. It's enormous and is the same size as downstairs. I'm thinking we knock down the dividing wall and open it up. We can build a bedroom or three in the back, put in a full kitchen, and add tons of windows and a skylight. We can even insulate the floor and make it soundproof."

Preacher studied his Hummingbird as she took in the space. He knew most girls wouldn't want this, but he was hoping she, like him, was a bit different. She walked over to a small back window, rubbed at the dirty glass, and peered out. He knew she could see the cabins and the lake from the window and he sighed. She'd made her decision.

"Can we build a large porch off the back?" she asked hesitantly. "Maybe we can sit out there and watch the sunsets. The view would be amazing."
Surprised, Preacher grabbed her and wrapped her in a tight hug. He laughed when she pulled back.

"We could have a wall of windows, maybe with French doors so we could enjoy the view. Oh, and I'd love a farmhouse sink." He couldn't help it, he threw back his head and laughed.

"I absolutely love you Hummingbird," he chuckled. "You were made for me."

Then he stopped laughing when her stupid flip phone rang.

Chapter Thirty Three
Macy

Macy opened her phone and peered at the screen. When she saw it was her dad, she looked at Preacher as she answered it.

"Dad?" she said in surprise.

"Macy," came his obviously panicked response. "Pike knows where you are."

"What?" she whispered in complete shock.

"He got me. Took my phone and traced your number. I got it back, but he's gearing up to head your way," her dad told her.

Macy listened closely. His breathing was ragged and his speech was choppy.

"What's wrong with you?" she cried. "You sound hurt."

"I delivered half the money. He wouldn't take it. He only wants you now. He hurt me pretty bad Macy," he rasped.

Macy immediately looked at Preacher as tears started to fall. He was already alert and had his phone to his ear. She concentrated on her own call though and ignored his.

"Where are you?" she asked as she trembled.

"I'm almost to you," her dad told her. "I should reach the gates in about five minutes."

"How bad?" she whispered. She could hear him sigh, and then he took a big breath.

"It's bad baby," he told her.

Macy turned then and flew down the stairs. She could hear Preacher yelling her name as he gave chase, but she didn't stop. She crashed into the door at the bottom of the stairs and shook off the pain in her shoulder. Reaching out, she twisted the handle and pushed it open. Then she was running down the hall.

"Macy," she heard whispered into the phone.

"I'm coming," she yelled, as she ran into the common room. All the bikers stopped and stared at her, but she didn't even see them. "You hold on," she cried.

Macy ran through the room and straight to the door that led outside. Preacher was still behind her and calling her name, but there was a whole room between them. She reached for the door knob, but before she could touch it a hand landed there first. She turned her head and found herself staring at her brother.

"It's dad," Macy cried. Then she shoved the phone in Snake's hand and pushed out the door. She wasted no time tearing across the compound and heading for the gates. She could hear tons of booted feet pounding on the pavement behind her, and she could only assume every biker there had followed her out.

When she could see the gates, she started screaming. "Open the gates." She continued to scream as her feet took her closer and closer. Macy had almost reached them when they finally started to open. She slipped through the tiny opening and ran straight into the middle of the road. She then turned in the direction she had come from that first night and would have started running again, but massive arms closed around her.

Macy struggled. She kicked and flailed as she tried desperately to free herself. Suddenly her brother was in her face.

"He's almost here. Calm down little sister," Snake told her. She was thankful he still had her phone pressed to his ear. And she knew it was Preacher that held her so carefully.

"Give me the phone," she demanded. As she tugged one of her arms free.

Then they finally heard a car approaching and everyone stopped to stare down the road. It was headed their way at a fast clip, and it was swerving all over the road.

"Oh my god," Macy cried as she saw how out of control the car was.

"Everyone get safely behind the gates," Preacher bellowed. Then her feet left the ground as Preacher lifted her and ran back inside the gates.

"No," Macy cried as she turned her head, trying to keep her eyes on the car.

It took only a few minutes for the car to make its way down the rest of the road. Then she heard a terrible crash. One side of the gates buckled as her dad missed the opening and crashed right into it. When it was obvious, the car wasn't going anywhere, the bikers took off again, running flat out for the car. Her only relief came when she saw Snake in the lead. He'd get to their dad first.

"I need to go to him," Macy pleaded as she sobbed.

Preacher didn't let go though, and she watched as Snake opened the car door and dragged their father out. Even from a distance she could see the blood that coated his skin and clothes. She threw her elbow back and knew from the pain she felt that she connected with Preacher's face. Immediately he let her go.

"Motherfucker," Preacher growled. But she didn't stop to see what damage she'd done to his already battered face. She took off once more and ran for the group of bikers surrounding her father.

Chapter Thirty Four
Preacher

Preacher tried to keep a hold of his hysterical Hummingbird, but the elbow she threw at him fucking hurt. His face was already throbbing, now he'd have another bruise to add to the growing collection. He let her go the minute she connected, and now she was tearing down the road towards her father's car.

Preacher sighed and started running after her again. He had to admit, the tiny girl was fucking fast. She'd give Trike a run for his money. She reached the car and pushed through the bikers. Preacher noticed Snake had got Wes out, and the man was lying on the road.

Instead of elbowing his way through the brothers, he bellowed "move" and a path immediately opened for him. Macy was already on the ground and had her father's head in her lap. Snake was hunkered down beside her, with Sniper, Raid and Shadow surrounding them. They had his shirt ripped open, but there was so much blood, Preacher wasn't even sure the man was alive.

"How bad?" he questioned, as his eyes looked over his girl. She was sobbing and already covered in her dad's blood.

"Don't know?" Shadow answered. "But there's a lot of blood. Too much blood," he added. "We fucking need Doc."

"I'm here," Doc called out as he pushed through the brothers. "Jesus," he grunted when he got a look at Wes.

Doc immediately opened his medical bag and got to work. The first thing he did was pat down his stomach and chest.

"Two broken ribs, possibly three," Doc relayed. When he moved to the sides he stopped. "Shit," he growled. "Looks like he was stabbed on his right side." He turned to Raid and asked for help. "Try to stop the bleeding. I need to find any other injuries."

Preacher moved to Macy and crouched down at her side. She immediately leaned into him and let him take her weight. He didn't wipe her tears or lie to her and tell her everything would be okay. He just gave her his silent support.

"Another stab wound to his leg, and it looks like his left arm is broken," Doc continued. Then he turned his eyes to Macy. "I need you to let go darling. I need to check his neck and head."

"I don't want to let go," Macy cried, causing Doc looked at her sympathetically.

"I know," Doc soothed. Then he nodded at Preacher. Preacher hated that he was going to have to physically remove her. He reached for her, but suddenly Snake was there. He crouched behind her, wrapped his arms around her stomach and pulled her back.

"Come on little sister. We need to move a bit so dad can get the help he needs," Snake insisted gently. She sagged back, and Preacher hoped like hell it didn't hurt her back.

"Preacher," Macy cried out in obvious panic, as she latched onto his hand.

"I'm right here Hummingbird," Preacher assured her. "I'll stay right by your side." She nodded, then looked back down at her dad.

"We need to get him to the hospital," Doc ordered. "The stab wound is deep and I can't tell if it's done any damage internally. Also, he's got a bad gash on his head that's got me concerned."

"I've got it covered," Preacher informed him. Then he smirked when a van came barreling down the road towards them. "Right on time."

It pulled up as close to them as it could get, then the doors opened and Mario and Trent jumped out.

"You need a ride?" Mario inquired as he opened the back doors.

Raid, Shadow and Sniper carefully lifted Wes' body up, and placed him in the back of the van. Then they all jumped in, along with Doc. When Macy went to try to get in too, Preacher stopped her.

"They won't have enough room to work," Preacher told her. Then he pointed to the SUV that was barrelling towards them. "I've got Smoke coming to give us a ride. We can follow right behind them."

Macy watched as Trent closed the doors and got back in. In seconds they were off, and then Preacher was gently pulling her towards the SUV.

"Snake, you're with us. The rest of you lock down the compound. I want to be ready if Pike shows up," Preacher ordered.

He helped Macy in the back, while Snake climbed in the front. Once he was in as well Smoke took off. Things had just turned serious, and Preacher was ready to do what he needed to keep his girl safe.

Chapter Thirty Five
Macy

Macy sat in the backseat with Preacher, crying and clinging to him, as they raced to the hospital. Her dad looked bad, and his condition frightened her. Preacher silently held her, and she was grateful. She appreciated his strength, and she appreciated the fact that he didn't tell her everything would be okay. She understood this could end bad.

Macy looked in the mirror and caught her brother's worried expression as he watched her. She could see the pain on his face as clear as her own, but he was thankfully holding strong. She reached over the seat, and immediately he turned slightly so he could reach back and engulf her hand in his own. They stayed like that the rest of the way to the hospital.

As soon as Smoke got close to the entrance, Snake let go of her hand, threw the door open and jumped out. He was inside the doors before she even had a chance to get out of the SUV. Preacher wrapped his arm around her shoulders and guided her through doors and across the lobby. Snake was half in the elevator and holding the doors open with his massive body.

When Macy reached him, she stood on her tiptoes, kissed his cheek, then stepped inside. She was surprised to see the man that had been in the passenger seat of the van already there. He was wearing jeans, dress shoes, a dress shirt and suit jacket.

"Are you a biker?" Macy asked curiously.

"I'm a business man," he chuckled. "I'm a part of the club, but I don't wear the vest."

"Mario," she said, as she recognized Alex's description of him. "You and Alex are together."

"That's my Angel," he confirmed as his eyes lit up. Then he turned serious. "Doc took your dad into surgery right away. He had some internal injuries that needed immediate attention. He also had a head wound that Doc was concerned about. He said we could sit in the waiting room, and to warn you the surgery could take hours."

"Okay," she whispered, as more tears ran down her cheeks. "So we wait."

Snake grabbed her hand and smiled down at her. "He's going to be okay little sister. Dad's a fighter, and you know he can weasel his way out of any situation. He'll get out of this one and then laugh at us for worrying."

Finally the elevator doors opened and Mario led them down a hall and into a small room. She was surprised to see Shadow, Sniper, Raid, and who she realized was Trent, already inside.

They nodded at her as Preacher took a seat, then pulled her down on his lap. It was an hour before there was a sudden commotion in the hall.

"Let go of my arm, I'm fine," they heard being yelled.

"You've only just been released," was growled back.

Then Misty was barging in the room with Trike on her heels. She walked straight to her brother and handed over Brady. He smiled at her, then sat and stared at his nephew. The next thing Macy knew, Misty was converging on her.

"Oh Macy, I'm so sorry about your dad," Misty cried. Then she turned to Trike. "Please Brody, can you go ask a nurse for a spare pair of scrubs? We need to get Macy cleaned up." Trike nodded and hurried out the door.

"Come on Macy. Let's go to the bathroom and see if we can fix you up a bit. Preacher can stand guard outside the door and bring in the clean clothes when Brody comes back. And Snake can stay here in case there's news," Misty ordered.

"But," Macy tried, but she was cut off.

"My babies fine with his uncle, and it won't take us long. I'll leave as soon as I know you're comfortable," Misty promised.

"I got him Monkey," Sniper said. "Go do your thing."

"You taking over the club honey?" Preacher smirked, as he raised a brow at Misty.

"No, I'm just stealing your girl for a minute," she chuckled. "Give us ten, then you can barge in and take her back."

Then without waiting for an answer, Misty took her hand and led her away. Ten minutes later Macy knew Misty was a true friend. The girl helped clean her up, dried her tears, and made her laugh. And all this was not even a day after giving birth.

True to his word, Preacher pushes in ten minutes later. She quickly changed, then watched as Misty retrieved her baby, got a kiss from her brother, and was led away by Trike.

It was three hours after that when Doc walked into the room.

Chapter Thirty Six
Preacher

Preacher immediately stood with his Hummingbird as Doc approached. Snake was right beside them, and it looked like he was trying to figure out from Doc's express how bad the news would be.

"It's not good," Doc informed them. "I've got him stabilized, but he had a couple of serious injuries. I'm in amazement he made it to the compound."

"Give us a rundown," Snake ordered.

Doc signed. "The minor injuries were things such as shallow cuts, bruising and three broken ribs."

"And the major," Preacher questioned as he pulled his girl closer into his side.

"His broken ribs punctured a lung and tore at some stomach tissue. It caused quite a bit of internal bleeding. He had a stab wound on his side that was deep. And, he had a cut high on his forehead that I've stitched," Doc explained.

"So it's his stomach injuries that are a concern?" Snake asked with a frown.

"No," Doc answered. "He has significant swelling on the back of his head. It looks like he took a serious blow to it. I've got him hooked up to an IV and I'm hoping that the medicine we get into him will reduce it."

"And if it doesn't go down?" Macy asked.

"Then it will restrict oxygen to his brain. But I don't want to jump to any conclusions until we have to. I'll stay and keep a close watch on him overnight. If we can get it down, it will take a while, but he should make a full recovery," Doc told them.

"Can I see him?" Macy asked.

"You three can go in, but he's unconscious. He'll probably stay that way until the swelling subsides. My advice is to spend a few minutes with him, then go back to the compound and rest. There's nothing you can do for him tonight," Doc advised.

"We'll go in together, and visit for a bit, but I'm leaving some of the brothers here for protection. If Pike comes this way, I don't want anything to happen to him," Preacher replied.

"I'm staying too," Snake growled. "But take my sister back and get her cleaned up. I want that clubhouse locked down, and I need you to stay by her side."

"The brothers are taking care of it as we speak, and there's enough brothers still here to cover us on the ride back. We'll go back in the SUV so she won't be out in the open," Preacher promised. He would have given him a beating for the way he was ordering him around, but because of Macy he let it go. The brother had a lot to deal with right now.

They followed Doc down the hall, and Preacher motioned for Sniper and Raid to follow. The brothers were partners in the marines, and they worked well together.

"Stay in the hall. Keep the guns I know you're carrying hidden, but if you need to use them don't hesitate. You get tired, you call Shadow and Navaho to relieve you," Preacher demanded. The brothers nodded and leaned against the wall on either side of the door.

Macy cried as soon as she stepped in the room, and Preacher had to admit Wes didn't look good. He was pale and had a million tubes running out of his body. That, and the bandages wrapped around his head, made him look like he was on the brink of death.

Preacher stood back and let Snake and Macy have a minute. Macy cried softly in her brothers arms for a while before she gathered the strength to lean down and give her father a quick kiss on the cheek. Preacher then led her away and left Snake in the room with their dad.

"I've got a cot being brought in for Snake. I know he won't use it, but it will be more comfortable than the chair," Doc told him, and Preacher nodded his thanks.

When they reached the waiting room again Mario stood.

"You'll ride with me and Trent in the SUV. Smoke can drive the van. The brothers headed down to start their bikes and move everything to the entrance. We should be able to walk outside and jump right in," Mario informed him.

"Appreciated," Preacher acknowledged. Then he turned his attention to Macy. "Let's get you back to the compound, showered and fed, then we can get you settled for the night. You're going to need some sleep Hummingbird."

"Yes McDreamy," Macy sighed as she leaned into him and gave him her weight. He smiled, but then lost it when he heard Mario snort from behind him.

"One word and I'm telling Alex you secretly hate wearing jeans and want your suit pants back," Preacher said.

"You wouldn't," Mario growled. "She loves me in jeans. I wear them for her."

"I know," Preacher smirked as he walked his Hummingbird out.

"Fucking president," Mario snarled as he followed them to the SUV.

Chapter Thirty Seven
Macy

When they arrived at the clubhouse, Macy let
Preacher help her out of the back of the SUV. He
slammed the door, rapped on the hood, and the car
sped off. She'd recently learned that Mario lived in a
massive log cabin that overlooked the other cabins.

Preacher opened the clubhouse door, and she was
led through the common room. She wasn't in the
mood for talk or sympathy, so she kept her eyes on
the floor. When Preacher stopped, she wasn't paying
attention and slammed into his back. When she
sheepishly looked up, he was looking down at her
with a worried expression.

"You okay Hummingbird?" Preacher questioned, as
he placed his thumb under her chin and tipped her

head up. All Macy could do was shrug her shoulders, and his frown deepened.

"You hungry?" Preacher questioned. When she shook her head he sighed. Then he turned to face the bar.

"Navaho," he called. She didn't look over, but she assumed the biker was there when Preacher continued. "Give us a couple hours, then bring us a plate of food we can snack on," he ordered.

"Will do," Macy heard the biker reply, then she was led back down the hall.

When they reached Preacher's door he stopped. It almost seemed like he didn't want to go in. His eyes closed, and he seemed to hold his breath. Then he quickly threw open the door. As she watched, he took one step inside, then slowly cracked one eye open. He peered around, and then the breath he had been holding whooshed out of him. He opened his other eye, then turned and pulled her inside.

Macy scanned the room, but she couldn't understand what he had been looking for. Whatever it was, he was relieved about it, and right now she really didn't care to ask.

"You trust me Hummingbird?" he asked as he looked down at her tenderly.

"I trust you Preacher," she whispered in return. He walked to the door, shut it, and turned the lock. Then he pulled her into the bathroom and shut that door too.

Seconds later warm water was pouring from the shower head and the room was steaming up. He moved towards her and slowly lifted the scrubs over her head, then pushed her pants down. She stood before him completely naked and moved to cover herself.

"Turn around," Preacher ordered. "I want to check your back."

She turned and waited a minute. She heard something tearing and sighed when her back was covered in Saran Wrap. She stayed that way for a minute until she calmed, then slowly turned back around. When she did, it was to see Preacher was stripped, and standing in the shower in nothing but a pair of boxers. She couldn't help staring at him a minute before climbing in herself.

While Macy watched, he took a sponge, lathered it with soap, and then slowly placed it on her skin. She sighed as he gently started to scrub at the remaining blood. She leaned against him and closed her eyes, as he carefully cleaned her from head to toe. His hands were warm and his touch was soothing. When he was done, he moved onto her hair, and she swore she was in heaven. Before she was ready the water was turned off, and he was drying her with a towel.

"I love you," Macy softly admitted. Preacher's eyes darkened and his face turned serious.

"I fucking love you too Hummingbird," he growled. "I always thought my club was the only thing I could ever love, but then you showed up. It feels like you were made to be mine."

"Then make me yours," she pleaded as she moved to the bed and laid down. When his facial expression only turned more intense, she blinked, then titled her head.

"Jesus, you're my kryptonite," he told her as he stripped out of his wet boxers, climbed on the bed, and covered her tiny body with his.

Macy closed her eyes as he kissed every part of skin he could reach. His warm hands roamed, and she had never felt so treasured. When he finally sank into her, she was ready and eager. He made love to her slowly, and carefully, and it was exactly what she needed. His love was obvious by the care he showed her.

Later they talked, cuddled, and snacked on the food Navaho had left outside the door. When she fell asleep, she curled up on him, and she realized that being with him made everything better.

Chapter Thirty Eight
Preacher

Preacher woke up and smiled. His Hummingbird was curled up tight against his side. Her head was cushioned on his shoulder, and her hand was resting over his heart. He vowed then and there he was waking up like this from now on.

He stroked her back lightly and was happy to see that it was looking better. The stitches were almost ready to come out, and the redness was starting to go away. It would still be awhile before it was better, but it was getting there. Preacher was relieved that making love to her last night hadn't done her any further damage. He had been extremely careful of her wounds.

After a few more minutes Macy began to stir. Preacher kissed the top of her head and waited for her to look up at him. Slowly her head titled back and her beautiful eyes locked on his. He watched as a pretty little blush spread across her cheeks.

"Morning Hummingbird," Preacher softly greeted.

"Morning Loverboy," she replied sleepily. Then she blinked and turned redder. He threw back his head and laughed as he pulled her closer.

"I think those names just pop out of your head," he remarked as he smirked at her. "You really have no filter for them."

"I'm sorry," Macy apologized as she ducked her head. "I'll try to stop."

Preacher grabbed her hair and gently tugged, forcing her eyes back.

"Don't you dare stop," he growled. Then he kissed her and made sure she knew how much he liked it. When he pulled back her eyes were closed, and she looked dazed.

"Okay," she whispered.

"Okay," he repeated. "Just so you know, you're waking up just like this every morning. Now that you're mine I'm not letting you go."

Macy opened her eyes again, and soft smile lit her pretty face. "I don't want you to let me go. I've never felt so comfortable and safe in my whole life," she revealed. "I feel loved."

"You are loved," Preacher growled. "And I'll make sure you know it every single fucking day." Her stomach growled then, and he chuckled.

"Time to get up, get dressed, and go get some breakfast," he ordered. "I'll take you back to the hospital afterwards, and we'll see how your fathers doing."

Macy's eyes turned sad and Preacher knew she was worried about him. He helped her out of bed, put more ointment on her back, and sent her in to do her thing in the bathroom. When she came out, he hurried through his bathroom routine, and then led her to the common room.

As soon as he stepped inside his eyes locked on Steele. He headed straight to the table his VP sat at. He grabbed a chair, sat, then pulled his Hummingbird down on his lap. She didn't complain at all, just curled up against his chest. A minute later Navaho placed two steaming plates of food in front of them.

"I've got word to Darren and Colin that Pike's headed this way. They're going to keep an eye out. Mario also said he'd have his men take some drives around town and keep an eye on things. And Trent's got his nose stuck in his laptop, so hopefully we'll know where he is soon," Steele I formed him.

Then Preacher watched Steele reach in his pocket and pull something out. "Mario said to give you this. It's all set up and should work like a charm," Steele told him. Preacher took it, then he turned to face Macy.

"We've had a few problems over the last little while, and we're working on doing some things to alleviate them. This is one," Preacher explained to his girl. He opened his hand and showed her the delicate Hummingbird charm he had put on a chain for her.

"It's beautiful," Macy cried as a tear slipped down her cheek.

"I bought this for you a while ago," Preacher admitted. "But I gave it to Mario so he could have Trent put a tracking device in it. I'm not saying anything will happen to you," he growled. "But if it does, I want to be able to get to you quickly." Macy nodded in understanding, so he took that as a yes and placed it around her neck.

"Thank you," she said quietly. Then she wrapped her arms around his neck and held on tight.

They sat like that for a few minutes, until his phone rang. Sighing in frustration, he pulled back, grabbed it, and checked the number. When he saw Shadow's name his body locked. He knew in his gut things were about to turn bad.

Chapter Thirty Nine
Macy

Macy leaned over so she could see Preachers phone too, and would know who was calling. When she saw it was Shadow she immediately became worried. The biker had left for the hospital not long ago and was with her father and brother. She looked at Preacher worriedly, and he grabbed her hand and squeezed in silent support, before answering his phone.

"Shadow," Preacher greeted. "You need to be relieved already. You only just got there, and Navaho will be headed over shortly." Preacher listened for a few minutes, and as Macy watched, his face got darker. She glanced around the table and noticed all the bikers were now alert and watching him.

"No sign at all?" Preacher pushed. Then he paused again. "How long?" he questioned. "No, stay there, I'm sending Trent to you. He can get into the security cameras. Me and some of the boys will head there as well."

When Preacher hung up, Macy pulled on his arm. When he turned to look down at her, he had a grim expression on his face.

"Pike got my father," she whispered, knowing that was what he was going to say.

"No Hummingbird," he denied. "Pike got your brother." Tears pooled in her eyes, and she shoved her face into his neck. His strong arms instantly wrapped around her.

"Steele, call Mario," Preacher ordered. "Tell him to grab Trent and his fucking laptop and meet us at the hospital. Dragon, call Darren and tell him and Colin to get there as well."

"Lucifer, take Smoke with you. Sweet talk the fucking nurses on every floor and see if they saw anything. Use that fucking charm and show your chest if you need to."

Lucifer smirked, but as Macy watched, he grabbed Smoke and headed to the door. She was happy to see Navaho and Tripp were right behind him.

"I'll get access to the tapes before Darren can," Tripp told him. "I know the security guys."

Macy leaned back and watched as Preacher nodded. He was in president mode, and she didn't want to disturb him.

"I want everybody locked and loaded," Preacher bellowed. "Sniper just got to sleep, but wake his ass up and get him on the roof. Tell Raid to join him when he gets here. I don't expect Pike to head this way, but I'm not taking chances with the woman and children. Get them all up to the fortress."

Finally, Preacher turned his eyes to her. Macy wiped at her tears as she looked up at him.

"You're sticking with me Hummingbird," he ordered. "We're headed to the hospital, and I don't want you out of my sight."

Macy immediately nodded. She knew the safest place was with him, but she couldn't help worrying about Snake. Preacher held her hand, and she followed as he led her out of the clubhouse and over to his bike. In minutes, he had helped her with her helmet, and she was on the back of his Harley. He gave her leg a squeeze then pulled out of the gates.

As they hit the road, she noticed Steele and Dragon had pulled up on either side of them. She turned back and saw several other bikes were behind her as well. She didn't recognize them all, but she knew there were bikers she hadn't met yet.

When they reached the hospital, the entire group pulled right up to the doors. The security guards glared at them, but they didn't say a word. Preacher got her helmet off quickly, stored it away, then they all headed inside.

When they reached the door to her fathers room, Macy was surprised to see so many people there. It looked like Trent had just arrived with his laptop, because he was opening it up. Tripp came hurrying down the hall with a jump drive in his hand. Darren and Colin had just arrived and were questioning Shadow, and if she was right, Dagger was leaning against the wall holding a stick of dynamite.

"Is that dynamite?" Macy asked Preacher, as she pointed to Dagger. Preacher glanced the bikers way and nodded.

"It is," he told her, without a hint of concern.

Macy would have question it further, but suddenly somebody bellowed her name. She'd know that voice anywhere, even with how weak it sounded. She let go of Preacher's hand and hurried into her fathers room, thankful that he was finally awake. She knew Preacher had things handled, and she prayed Snake would come home safe.

Chapter Forty
Preacher

When Wes called Macy's name, she bolted from Preacher's arms and ran into his. Preacher took the time to discuss things with Mario.

"I want to know how Pike got Snake out of here, and I want to see what the fucker looks like," Preacher ordered.

"Right," Mario replied. "Trent's got the security footage now, thanks to Tripp. He should have something shortly. I've got half my men searching, and the other half guarding the woman and children."

Preacher nodded and turned to Steele next. "You find out anything, you get your ass in that room and you let me know."

Steele nodded and turned back to finish his conversation with Darren and Colin.

"Put that dynamite away," Preacher ordered Dagger as he ran his hands through his hair in agitation. "You're creeping out the staff."

Dagger snickered, but he did as asked. Preacher sighed, then headed into the room his Hummingbird was in. He found her huddled close to her father and studying all his wounds.

"I'm fine," Wes was insisting. "The doctor said the swelling is going down."

"You almost died," Macy whispered.

Preacher stepped forward then and crowded his Hummingbird. As soon as he did, Wes glared at him.

"You move fast boy," he sneered.

"I do when I see the girl I plan on spending the rest of my life with," Preacher returned.

"You going to keep her safe?" Wes questioned with a bite to his voice.

"I will put her life before mine if I need to," Preacher growled.

Wes nodded. "You got questions boy, ask away. The drugs they got me on keep me knocked out pretty good. Don't figure I'm going to be awake long."

Preacher nodded, then sat in the chair Snake had used and pulled his Hummingbird down on his lap.

"What happened?" Preacher immediately asked.

"Got half the money, not going to tell you how, and decided half was better than nothing. Took it to Pike. Pike explained the deal was off. Said all he wanted was my daughter. Course, I didn't agree with that. Got the beating for it," Wes explained.

"How the hell did you get out of there?" Preacher asked curiously.

"Played possum. When the guards figured I was done, I crawled the fuck out. Pike had got a hold of my phone. He found where I'd hid Macy. Headed straight here. I may not be the best dad, but I can sure as fuck hold a gun," Wes grunted.

Preacher could see Wes' eyes were getting heavy, and he knew the man was almost out again.

"What happened to Snake?" he questioned.

"Don't know," Wes huffed. "I only just woke up. Didn't even know he spent the night in here with me." Preacher nodded in understanding.

"You get my girl out of here. You get her back to the compound. You protect her like the fucking biker president I know you are," Wes ordered, then as Preacher watched, the man closed his eyes and was out.

"Let's go Hummingbird," Preacher ordered. "You heard the man." He didn't wait for a reply, he grabbed her hand and pulled her from the room.

"Steele, you got anything?" Preacher questioned as they approached his VP.

"Footage shows a man in a doctors coat pushing a gurney out the front doors. Snake's on the gurney," Steele relayed. "And he isn't moving."

"I'm getting Macy out of here. I need you to get us back safely," Preacher demanded.

"Let's go" Steele agreed.

Preacher moved down the hall, but took the stairs. The brothers followed. He wasn't wasting time waiting for the three elevators it would take to get them all down. When they reached the main floor they moved out of the stairs and headed for the door.

They almost made it out when a doctor blocked their way. Before Preacher could react, he found a gun placed at his head. Immediately every brother there pulled their own gun and aimed it at the doctor.

"Pike I assume?" Preacher growled, as he tried to push Macy towards Dragon. Pike's hand shot out and grabbed his Hummingbird before she even moved.

"Not so fast," Pike growled as he pulled Macy back. Preacher fumed knowing he couldn't do a thing. The fucker was using his girl as a shield.

"Shoot the fucker?" he ordered.

Preacher watched as both Shadow and Sniper moved. The two men raised their guns, but before they could move, Pike gave him a hard shove Then he heard the unmistakable sound of a gun firing. Preacher felt a burning on the side of his head before he fell.

Preacher lay there blinking for a minute, and could only watch as his Hummingbird lost it. He knew she was screaming, but he couldn't hear her. Finally everything went dark, and he had no way to fight it.

Chapter Forty One
Macy

Macy felt her whole body shatter, when the gun fired, and Preacher went down. Blood was pouring out of the side of his head, and he wasn't moving. She screamed as she felt herself break, and would have gone down if not for Pike's Tight hold on her. She didn't struggle, she just stared straight at Preacher. Bikers were yelling, and Macy finally realized Pike had the gun to her head.

"Put the fucking guns down," Pike screamed. "I shot the big guy, I won't hesitate to shoot Macy."

"Do as he says," Steele ordered, taking charge. "If he shoots her, we're all dead men."

Macy saw movement and assumed the bikers were doing what Steele said, but she refused to take her eyes off Preacher. She was still sobbing when Pike dragged her to the door.

"You're a fucking dead man," Dragon growled. "And I can't wait until I introduce you to my blowtorch."

Pike stumbled in obvious fear, then he was moving again. Macy screamed louder as she started to lose sight of Preacher. When he was completely out of view she felt like she was dying herself.

"They'll follow," Macy cried as Pike dragged her towards a car.

"I've been standing outside for hours," Pike sneered. "Every car or bike that pulled up got their tires slashed. No one's fucking following us." He opened the door of the car they were standing beside and pulled a zip tie from his pocket.

"Hands," he ordered.

When Macy simply stared at him he smacked her hard, and she fell against the side of the car. When he repeated his order a second time, she had no choice except to do as told. Her hands were quickly secured together, and he shoved her in the car.

Minutes later they were out of the parking lot and headed out of town.

"Did you kill my brother?" Macy asked fearfully. When Pike twisted to look at her and chuckled, she felt more tears fall.

"He's alive for now, but I'm not sure how long I'm going to let him stay that way," he snickered.

"Why me?" Macy questioned, not understanding his fixation.

"You were the prettiest girl in school. I used to watch you, and I fucking wanted you. But every time I asked you out you said no. That one time I caught you outside the locker room I thought I had you. When I touched you, your skin was so soft. But then you screamed, and I heard people coming. You got lucky that day," Pike told her.

"But you had other chances," Macy said with some confusion. "You never went after me again."

"Because your fucking brother put me in the god damned hospital for a week," Pike bellowed.

Macy suddenly realized the car was slowing down. It finally stopped in the middle of the woods, hidden from view by tall, dense trees. Pike climbed out and moved around the car, opened her door, and pulled her out too. She stumbled several times as he dragged her through the woods. After a few minutes he stopped and let her go.

"Move and I'll kill you," Pike snarled.

Then Macy watched in horror as he kicked some leaves out of the way. When Pike bent, she saw a handle sticking out of the ground. He tugged it and a hidden door opened.

"Moonshiners used to use this area," informed her as he pushed her down a set of dark stairs. "I figure this is one of their old hideouts."

Macy reached the bottom and assumed she was in a basement of some sort. Pike pushed her down a long dirty hall. Macy noticed rooms were on either side, but Pike didn't stop until he reached the end of the hall. He then removed a key from his front pocket and unlocked the door.

When Macy looked inside she was horrified to see a metal cot and absolutely nothing else. Pike spun her around, pulled a knife from his pocket, and cut the zip ties.

"Welcome to your new home," he laughed as he shoved her inside. "You'll stay here for three days.

At the end of those days I'll be back, and when I come back, you and me are going to finish what I started that day outside the locker room."

Then the door was slammed shut and Macy found herself sealed in. She moved to the dirty cot and sat down. She didn't care about herself, all she hoped was that her dad, Snake, and Preacher were okay. Macy lay down on the dirty mattress and curled into a ball. All she could do now was sob for the biker president she loved.

Chapter Forty Two
Preacher

The room was dark but Preacher could hear voices. The main voice he caught was Steele's, and that settled him a bit, but he knew something was terribly wrong. He tried to remember what had happened, but his fucking head was pounding and he couldn't concentrate.

Preacher cracked open an eye and peered around the room. He saw Steele, Mario, Tripp, Dragon, Shadow and Tiffany. He closed his eye again and sighed. After a minute he opened them both up and almost fell off the bed. His god damned sister's face was about an inch from his.

"Jesus fucking Christ," Preacher roared, as he placed a hand against his chest. "What the fucks wrong with you?"

"Me," Tiffany yelled as she stared at him in horror. "You're the idiot that got shot in the head."

Preacher could only stare at her as he tried to remember what had happened.

"Someone shot you in the head," she suddenly wailed, then the tears started to fall as she lost it. Immediately he was squished, as she climbed on the bed on threw herself at him.

Preacher held her close, ignoring the pain in his ribs, and kissed the top of her head. She cried for a few minutes then pushed away, hauled back her fist, and punched him in the chest.

"What the fuck?" he yelled at her as he tried to rub the pain away.

"Don't you ever get shot in the head again," she yelled at him furiously.

Preacher couldn't do anything for a minute, trying to work out her mood swings. When he turned to Shadow in confusion, the biker shrugged.

"She's pregnant," Shadow offered in explanation. Then he moved across the room, grabbed Tiffany around the waist, and hauled her off his bed.

"Come on baby girl. Let's give the man with the head injury a minute," Shadow calmly requested. Then Preacher watched as Shadow sat in the chair beside the bed and placed Tiff on his lap.

Steele approached the bed next. "What do you remember?" he questioned.

Preacher ignored the pain for a minute and thought about what his sister had said. She said someone had shot him. Suddenly everything came rushing back. Pike kidnaping Snake. Him and Macy at the hospital. And finally, Pike grabbing Macy and shooting him in the head.

"Where the fuck's my girl?" Preacher bellowed as he sat bolt upright in bed. He swayed for a minute and Steele stepped towards him, but he waved the brother back.

"Pike took her," Dragon interrupted. "Held the gun to her head and after he shot you. We weren't risking her. Pike out the door using her as a shield."

"Fucking fuck," Preacher roared. "Get Trent in here with his god damned laptop."

"The tracker isn't working," Trent related from the floor in the corner. Preacher turned his way and lost it.

"Why the fuck not?" he roared. "I thought you were good at this shit."

Trent stared up at him, as he pushed off the floor angrily. "I am fucking good at this," he growled. "He either found it and got rid of it, or he has her somewhere where the god damned thing can't work."

"And let me guess," Preacher sneered. "None of you fuckers have found Snake either?" When nobody answered, he shoved off the bed and got in Steele's face.

"Get men out there searching." Then he turned to Trent. "Hack into traffic cams, do whatever you have to. Find the last spot you got a signal." Trent nodded and sat back down, so Preacher turned back to Steele.

"How long have I been out?" he questioned.

"About three hours," Steele replied.

"How bad is my fucking head?" Preacher asked next.

"Bullet grazed you. You now have eight stitches on the side of your head," Steele told him.

"Fine," Preacher grunted. "Find me some fucking pain medicine and lets fucking go." Then he twisted and headed for the door.

"Hey badass," his sister yelled. Preacher sighed as he stopped and turned to her. "Your fucking ass is hanging out."

Preacher glanced down and saw he was wearing a fucking hospital gown. And his ass was indeed hanging out.

"Why did they take my clothes when I just needed a couple stitches?" he growled at the group in general. Then he grabbed the back of the gown and held it shut.

"Because they had to do a CAT scan on your head you idiot," Tiffany yelled, then she burst out crying again.

Preacher ignored her and continued stomping out the door. Hospital gown or not, he was going after his girl, and fucking gutting Pike.

Chapter Forty Three
Macy

Macy lay on the cot and frowned. She had no idea
how long she had been in her prison, but she
assumed it had been three days. With no windows it
was hard to judge the passing time. She had a sick
feeling Pike would be back soon.

The time had passed painfully slow, and it hadn't
been kind to her. Pike had only left her a small
amount of water, and Macy knew she was hitting a
dangerous low. She was extremely weak, and all she
wanted to do was sleep.

Unfortunately, that was only the beginning of her
problems. She was in a basement, with only a tiny
lightbulb to give off light, but even she could see how
pale her skin had become. The room was
unbelievably damp, and the floor was dirt. It also

had no heating. Her jeans and tee hadn't been much protection. The cold had seeped right through them.

The worst thing though, was her back. The floor was dirt, the walls were rough stone, and the cot was dusty. Macy's back hadn't been tended to since she left, and she knew the bandages were dirty. She had tried to sleep on her side, but it hadn't helped.

Her back now felt like it was on fire, and she knew what that meant. Not only that, but even with how cold she was, she was bathed in a thin layer of sweat. Macy knew without a doubt her back was infected. With that, the cold temperatures, and no food or water, she understood things were taking a turn for the worst.

Macy had been in the hospital so many times she knew how much her body could take before it broke down. And she also knew she was way past that point.

During the first couple hours she had held onto her necklace and prayed that somebody would come. But as time passed, she knew her chances were getting slimmer and slimmer. Either Preacher had died from the bullet to his head, or because she was underground, the signal couldn't get through. She prayed it was the second option.

Macy knew Snake was down here somewhere with her, but she hadn't heard him, nor had she seen him on the way in. He was a big guy and he wouldn't have been easy to take down. If he was here, he must be badly hurt. She refused to think he could be dead. If either Snake or Preacher were dead, she hoped she died down here too.

Then Macy got to thinking, if Snake was down here and she died, he'd die too if he wasn't already dead. She also figured she had to be outside for the tracker to work. She was a biker president's girl, so she decided it was time she started acting like it. Macy gritted her teeth and forced herself to sit up. The room spun, but she pushed through it. She stood, but her knees gave way and she collapsed to the ground.

Macy was weaker than she thought, and she knew the infection must have moved to her chest. She growled as she pushed off the ground and got herself off the dirt floor. Then she moved back into a sitting position. She almost cried in happiness when she saw what was only about two inches from her face. The entire top of the cot was made of hundreds of large springs.

Macy braced herself against the side of the cot and pushed the mattress over a bit. She sighed in relief, pleased that Pike had given her such a decrepit cot.

The springs were loose, and several were almost completely unhooked. It took her ten minutes, but she wiggled one back and forth until the damn thing came free.

Macy looked down at the tight coil, and the long straight piece at the end that held a hook. The coil fit perfectly in her tiny fist, leaving the straight end with the hook sticking out. She hid it under the top corner of the mattress where it was easily within reach and then laid back down.

In minutes Macy had fallen asleep, but she did it with a smile on her face. She finally had the love she always dreamed of, and she wasn't letting Pike take that from her.

Chapter Forty Four
Preacher

Preacher was losing his ever loving mind. It was the third day since Pike took his Hummingbird, and he wasn't handling it well. Brothers were staying out of his way, and Steele kept telling him to get a lock on his anger. If his VP said that one more time, he was going to show him exactly how locked down his anger was, and it was going to hurt.

Preacher was tired, he was angry, and he was being an ass. He knew it, but he didn't care. He had found the one he was supposed to spend the rest of his life with and fucking Pike was trying to take her away. He was ready to pound the fucker, but he couldn't because he couldn't find him, and it was pissing him off.

Preacher had apologized to his sister though. He found out she was pregnant after just waking up in the hospital. He had been hurting, and his only thoughts had been for Macy. He gently pulled Tiff aside yesterday, held her tight, and told her how happy he was for her. Preacher was actually over the moon about becoming an uncle. She kissed him and told him he could make it up to her by buying her lots of baby gifts. He also congratulated Shadow, and they had shared a drink together.

Unfortunately, even though Preacher fucking wanted another one, that was the only drink he allowed himself to have. He needed his head on straight, and he needed to be able to ride at any given time. He was also refusing pain meds, and his head wasn't too happy with him about that.

Trent had been able to trace the tracker to a general location, but it was useless with all the trees around. It was in the middle of fucking nowhere, and the only thing they found was a ton of tire tracks. Of course a lot of the local teens used the woods for partying and bonfires, so that wasn't very helpful. Navaho tried to track, but even he said it was too well used to find a decent trail.

The tracker was still off line, and until it came back on, they were basically fucked. Brothers had been going out in pairs to search for his girl, but they always came back without her. Trent had also tracked Pike's car using the traffic cams, but once it hit the country roads, it was impossible to trace.

Doc was worried about his Hummingbird's back. Apparently if it wasn't kept extremely clean, she could get an infection. And from what Snake had told him, that wasn't something she could easily overcome.

Preacher picked up a bottle of whiskey and threw it against the wall. He was done with sitting around. He was going after his girl. He stomped furiously to the door, but was stopped by Steele.

"Where the fuck are you headed?" Steele growled, as he gripped down hard on Preacher's shoulder. Several other brothers had stood as well and were quickly approaching.

"I'm not fucking sitting here anymore. I'm going back to the woods, and I'm going to tear them apart until I fucking find her. That trackers going to light up again, and I plan on being there when it does," he snarled.

"Well okay," Steele easily replied. "Lets fucking go." Stunned, Preacher just stared at him.

"You don't fucking think you're going by yourself?"
Steele chuckled. "More men, more pairs of eyes.
Plus we're all itching for some action."

Preacher watched in stunned silence, as the whole
fucking room emptied. He shook his head and
headed for his bike. When he pulled out of the
compound, he wasn't surprised to see Smoke
following in a van, and Mario and his men following
in several cars. He had a god damned army with
him.

As he rode, he smiled for the first time in days. Pike
wasn't going to know what fucking hit him. Then he
turned his head when Dagger pulled up beside him.
He almost fell off his Harley when he got a look at his
brother's bike. The ass had strapped one of the
rocket launchers to the side, and he was grinning like
a loon. Preacher couldn't help it, he fucking grinned
back.

Chapter Forty Five
Macy

Macy woke suddenly when the door was thrown open. She lifted her head just in time to see Pike pocket a key. She was so sick she could barely move, and that scared her.

"Honey, I'm home," Pike greeted as he smirked at her. "You ready to be mine?"

"No," she croaked. "I'm Preacher's." At her words Pike's smirk disappeared.

"The fucking biker," he snarled. "Your god damned brother turned into one, but he was always an idiot. I never expected him to do much with his life. He proved me right."

Pike moved closer, and she gasped when she got a look at him. When he dragged her down here he had been in perfect health. She was surprised to see he now sported a black eye and his neck was bruised. Pike saw where she was looking and he growled.

"Snake," he sneered. "I mistakenly thought he was still out. I won't make that mistake again."

"Snake's here?" Macy asked as she stared at him hopefully.

"Fuckers locked in a room at the end of the hall. He's chained up good now. When I finish making you mine, I'm going to take care of him once and for all," Pike grinned sadistically.

Macy instantly paled. She tried to reach up, but Pike was on her before she got the chance. His weight pushed her into the mattress, and she cried out from the pain in her back. She shoved at him, but he only laughed. Panicking, she struggled and cried.

Before Macy could stop it he had reached down and ripped her blouse. Somehow she managed to get her arm up, and she punched him right in the same spot he had the black eye. Pike roared in pain, hauled back, and returned the punch. She saw stars and fought the blackness that tried to pull her under.

Pike took advantage of that and pawed at her breasts. Macy screamed at the painful way he squeezed them. Then his attention moved to her jeans. She twisted and struggled, but he still managed to undo the button and get the zipper down. He shoved his hand inside and stared down in fascination at where it disappeared.

Macy tried to block out what he was doing, because she knew now was the time to move. She reached up, pulled back the side of the mattress, and reached under it. She kept here eyes on Pike as she searched for the spring she had hidden there. It took her a minute, but finally her hand touched the corner of it. That was all she needed, she reached up and wrapped her hand around it, then pulled it out.

Macy made sure her grip was tight, then she moved quickly. She screamed as she swung with all the strength she could muster and shoved the end of the spring into his side. Pike bellowed and reared back, pulling his hand out of her pants. He grabbed her wrist and pulled back, dislodging the spring. Then he leaned down and growled at her.

"You shouldn't have done that little girl," he snarled.

Then Pike let go of her wrist and pulled back his fist. Macy moved before he could hit her, and reared up, shoving the spring into his right eye. Blood sprayed, and she watched in horror as he screamed and fell backwards. She wasted no time scrambling out from under him and rolling off the cot. As soon as her feet hit the floor she stood. She swayed and knew she was only running on adrenaline now.

Macy approached him cautiously, but he wasn't even looking at her. He rolled on the cot, cursing and swearing as he held the spring. She reached down and pulled the keys out of his pocket, then moved back out of his reach.

"You pull that out, you're going to pull your eye out with it," she warned him snidely, as she backed towards the door. "You hurt my family, and I want you to know that your death will be horrible. I'm locking you in, and my biker will be back to finish what I started," she promised.

Then Macy stumbled out the door and slammed it shut behind her just before he reached it. She didn't waste any time after that. She shoved the key in the lock and turned it, effectively sealing him in.

Chapter Forty Six
Macy

Macy stumbled down the dark hall, banging into the walls as she went. She knew the kick of adrenaline she had gotten while fighting Pike was wearing off. The cold stone seeped into her exhausted body every time she touched it. She had tried to hold her ripped blouse closed, but the effort it took to do that was too much now. She gave up and let go, putting all her strength into getting to the end of the hall.

Finally Macy reached a door she instinctively knew had to be the room her brother was in. She inserted the key into the lock and prayed the door would unlock. With a twist of her wrist, she heard the telltale click of the lock giving way. She used her weight to shove the door open and practically fell into the room.

The sight of Snake almost dropped Macy to her knees. Her brother was chained and hanging from a beam in the ceiling. The tips of his booted feet were the only parts of him that touched the floor. His bare chest was a mass of dark ugly bruises, and his face was bloody. He was completely unconscious.

Macy moved to his side as quickly as her body would allow her to and peered up at him. His shirt was missing, and so was his cut. She searched the room but didn't see them. Then as gently as she could she touched his stomach. She would have touched his face, but she couldn't reach it. Tears fell as she brokenly called out his name.

When Snake didn't react, she stared at his bloody chest. It was rising and falling steadily, which was a good sign. Macy had no idea what to do. There was no way she could reach the chains to get them off of him. Plus, in her weakened state, they were probably too heavy.

Desperate now, she leaned against him, and screamed up at him. "Snake, I need you." His eyes flew open, and he twisted and turned his head, most likely searching for her.

"Here," she whispered. "I'm right here," Macy cried as she wrapped her arms around his waist.

"Fucking Christ," Snake bellowed. "I never thought I'd see you again. How the hell did you get in here?" he growled. "And where the fuck is Pike?"

"Pike's locked in my cell," Macy told him as she peered up at him. "I got away, but I don't know how to get you free."

Snake eyed her closely. "You've got a lot of blood on you little sister and your sweating. How bad are you hurt?"

Macy backed away slightly, and he growled. "Did he rape you?"

"No," she hurried to assure him as she pulled her blouse back together. "And the blood is his."

"You've got a fever," he correctly guessed. "You need a hospital now."

"I need to figure out how to get you out of here," she told him, as she leaned against him again. She was weakening quickly now and was starting to panic.

"You get your ass out of here," Snake demanded. "If Preacher hasn't come, it's because he can't track you." She eyed him in surprise.

"I know about the god damned tracker and I agree with it. The stone walls must be blocking the damn signal. You move and get outside. He'll find you."

"I can't leave you," Macy sobbed, as she wrapped herself around him once more.

"You can," Snake sighed. "You're sick again little sister. It's obvious you could pass out at any minute. I love you for wanting to help, but if you pass out down here Preacher won't be able to find either of us. If you want to save me, you have to get out yourself."

Macy understood his logic, but she didn't like it. She kissed his bruised stomach then stepped away from him. Slowly, she stumbled to the door. Right before she left, she looked back at him.

"Proud of you little sister?" Snake called, then she turned away and headed for the stairs. She wouldn't let him down.

It took her what seemed like hours, to make her way up. When she pushed open the door, the sun felt like it was burning her eyes. She cried as she stumbled away from the prison.

Macy walked for a bit then collapsed against a large tree. She'd done her part, now Preacher needed to do his she thought as she closed her eyes. She prayed she wouldn't have to wait long.

Chapter Forty Seven
Preacher

Preacher pulled up to the spot they had stopped at before and shut off his Harley. The first thing he noticed was the car parked there. He climbed off his bike and moved closer to it.

"That's the car from the security cameras at the hospital," Trent confirmed as he moved up beside him. "The one the ass that took your girl was driving."

Preacher's back went straight. "So he's fucking here. That means my Hummingbird is here, and hopefully Snake too."

He then took off at a fast clip and powered through the woods. He could hear the brothers behind him cursing, and then the ground shook as everyone ran after him.

"Hey," Dagger grunted as he reached him first. "You keep running this fast, you're going to fall and break your fucking face."

Preacher threw up his middle finger and kept going. A minute later a body hit his back, and he was tackled to the ground. He flipped and raised his elbow, ready to take out whoever had pulled that stunt, when a fist hit his jaw first. He growled as he spit out blood.

"Stop and think you ass," Steele yelled from above him. "You don't even know which direction to go in. Give Trent a minute, and we'll see if he can bring something up on the computer."

"My girls here somewhere," Preacher snarled back.

"Yeah, and some of us have gone through this before," Dragon told him. "You told us all to calm down and think things through, so that's what we're telling you."

Besides, this isn't real stealthy like," Dagger added. "We sound like a god damned herd of elephants."

"Well that's because you're all following me," Preacher yelled back.

"Jesus Christ," Lucifer interrupted. "You followed me when the compound was attacked, and Blood's brother ran in with grenades."

"And you followed me when the outlaws took my Dewdrop again," Dragon growled.

"And you helped dig Misty out of a mine with your bare hands," Trike added.

"You helped us all," Shadow declared. "You can't expect us not to follow you. We're family."

Preacher hung his head. "Okay, so is there a signal?" he questioned, as Trent and Mario walked forward. Steele held out his hand, and Preacher took it. He was back on his feet in seconds.

"I'm getting a faint blip," Trent said with obvious surprise. They all moved at once and tried to huddle around the computer. As they watched, the blip got brighter. "Jesus, I think we've got her," Trent grinned. Preacher studied the map for a second then he was off again.

"For Christ's sake," Dagger yelled. "Did you not learn anything from the first tackle?"

Preacher ignored him and kept going. His girl had been gone for three days and he needed to find her. When he got close to the area, the map pinpointed he stopped. Trent was soon beside him again.

"She should be right over there by that tree," Trent said, as he pointed out a tall maple not too far away.

Preacher headed in that direction quickly. As soon as he got close, he could see his Hummingbird sitting on the ground. He sprinted the last few feet and dropped down beside her. She was unconscious and extremely pale. It was chilly out though, and she was sweating. Then he took in her ripped blouse and opened jeans.

"He fucking raped her," Preacher cried, as he rested his hand on her cheek.

"Relax hot stuff," his girl croaked. "I stopped him." Then her eyes popped open, and she smiled at him. "I missed you."

"Jesus," Preacher cried as he held her close. "I fucking missed you too Hummingbird."

"Snake's still in the basement," she whispered. "He's chained up, and I couldn't get him out. Pike's locked in a room, but he's got a sharp spring so he careful."

"Basement?" Wrench asked as he approached.

"There's a door in the ground, but I don't know if I can find it again," Macy cried.

"I can," Navaho immediately told them. Then he took off with about six brothers following him.

"You don't look too good sweetheart," Raid said, as he sat on the ground beside her.

"I think my back is infected, and I think I have pneumonia," Macy whispered. Then she closed her eyes again and fell to the side.

Preacher caught her before she hit the ground, scooping her up and rising quickly to his feet.

"She needs a hospital," he roared. "Snake warned me it's dangerous for her to get sick."

"Then lets get her out of here," Raid declared. "Doc's waiting with a SUV, and the brothers can follow with Snake."

"I'll take care of Pike," Mario added.

Preacher nodded and headed back to where they had left the bikes. He'd found her and she was safe in his arms, now he just needed her to be okay.

Chapter Forty Eight
Preacher

Preacher held his Hummingbird close all the way to the hospital. She didn't stir once, and he was concerned about her colour. She was way too pale, and the fine sheen of sweat covering her skin made him nervous. He had just gotten her back, he couldn't lose her now because of a cold or infection. Snake's warning kept ringing in his ears.

As soon as they reached the hospital Preacher was out, and Doc was waiting at the car door with a stretcher. Preacher glared at him as he ran passed him and into the hospital with his girl in his arms. Doc sighed and followed. He led Preacher down a hall, and as soon as they reached a room he pointed to a bed. Being as careful as he could, Preacher set her down, then let Steele drag him out and into a waiting room.

"She has to be okay," Preacher told his VP as he leaned forward and planted his elbows on his knees.

"She will be," Steele assured him. "The damn girl locked Pike in a room and found Snake. She's tough, even sick and in obvious pain she got herself out of there. She's definitely a girl worthy of you."

Preacher nodded in thanks. Even with Macy being so quiet, she had a strength about her he couldn't deny. She was damn perfect in every way.

About a half hour later, the rest of the bikers that hadn't come with them showed up. They were loud and caused quite a commotion.

"I can fucking walk," Preacher heard Snake yell.

"Well then stop banging off the walls and I'll let go of you," Wrench yelled back.

As soon as they entered the room, Preacher got a good look at Snake. The brother's face was a mess, he only wore pants, and his chest was a mass of bruises. He looked like shit.

"I think you need a Doctor," Preacher advised.

"I think I'll wait until I know my sisters okay," Snake shot back. "She came to the cell I was in and I got a look at her. The fucking pneumonia's back, so I'm not leaving until I hear how she is," he growled.

"Then sit the fuck down before you fall down, and let Raid look at you," Preacher ordered.

"Fine," Snake furiously agreed as he practically fell into the chair. As soon as he did Raid moved to his side.

"Ornery fucker," Preacher snorted, but all he got for that was a middle finger pointed his way. He would have laughed if he weren't so concerned about his girl.

"What's the story on Pike?" Preacher inquired. At that question, most of the brothers chuckled.

"Your girl deserves a medal," Lucifer finally explained. "Even fucking hurt she did you proud. Somehow got a spring loose. Shoved it in his side, then his eye."

"What?" Preacher said in stunned disbelief.

"He was screaming and rolling around on the floor," Wrench chuckled. "Ass was freaking. Spring was right through his right eye. We left it in and hauled him out of there. Apparently your girl told him if he took it out, he'd take the eye with it. He went nuts anytime we went near him."

Preacher was stunned. "Where's he now?" he questioned.

"Mario took him to the shed. Navaho went with them. They'll get him situated until you and Snake are ready," Dragon informed him.

"Fucking perfect," Preacher huffed in relief. His girl was surprising him more and more.

It was another hour before Doc came out. Preacher stood, but he wasn't surprised when Snake stayed seated. He gave the biker a break by leading Doc over to him. Raid had checked him out, and the fucker had two broken ribs. Other than that it was superficial wounds.

"Macy suffered some bruising and a few scrapes," Doc stated. "It also looks like she wasn't left any food or water. We ran an IV and are getting her on track. Her back is a mess. It's raw and quite infected. We've cleaned it up and are pumping her full of heavy antibiotics. She also has a fever, and it looks like she has developed pneumonia. She's unconscious, and we can't seem to wake her up," Doc explained.

Preacher dropped his head, and he heard Snake swear beside him. "So it's not good?"

"No," Doc confirmed. "But the next couple hours are critical. If she wakes up, it will be a good sign. If she doesn't, I fear the infection and pneumonia will cause her to slip into a coma. It's a waiting game now."

Snake stood and threw his chair against the wall. "I need some fucking air," he snarled as he pushed out of the room.

Preacher ignored him and turned to Doc. "I need to be with her," he demanded. Thankfully Doc nodded.

"I figured you'd say that. Follow me," Doc replied.

Preacher was pissed. He'd go in there and do whatever he could to wake her up. He definitely wasn't loosing her now.

Chapter Forty Nine
Preacher

Preacher had been dozing in the chair when his foot was kicked. He jerked awake and growled at the disturbance. Before even looking over to see who had done it, he looked at Macy. She was still lying there, covered in tubes and completely still. He sighed and looked up to find Dragon scowling down at him.

"What the fuck do you want?" Preacher asked his Sargent of Arms.

"You've been sitting here for over twenty-four hours. You need a break. Get your ass up and follow me," Dragon ordered. "We'll be back in an hour."

"I'm not fucking leaving," Preacher growled. "If it was Ali lying in this bed, you know fucking well you wouldn't leave either."

"No," Dragon immediately replied. "But then the brothers would just walk in here and drag my ass out, which is exactly what's going to happen if you don't play nice."

"I'd like to see you try," Preacher snorted in return.

"Fine by me," Dragon chuckled, as he put two fingers in his mouth and wolf whistled.

Preacher growled, as he found himself surrounded by Steele, Wrench, Shadow, Tripp and Sniper.

"Go," Snake advised from his position in a chair across the room. "I'm not in any shape to go on a road trip, and I don't fucking want to. If my sister wakes up, I'll make sure you know," he promised.

Preacher dropped his head in defeat, knowing damn well the brothers assembled would enjoy carrying him out of the hospital. And they wouldn't give a shit about the attention they'd get either.

"One hour," Preacher pushed as he glared at the lot of them. Then he rose and followed them out the door. The Harley's were parked right out front and his was there with them. He climbed on and pulled out of the parking lot, following his brothers down the road.

Fifteen minutes later, he was pissed to find himself back in the woods where his Hummingbird had been held. Dagger's bike was parked there, but he didn't give it a second thought as he glared at Steele.

"Why the fuck am I here?" Preacher growled.

"You need to see where Pike had her?" Steele told him. "Shut up and follow me."

Then Preacher watched as the brother headed into the woods. He gave up the fight and followed him. He had promised them an hour, so that's what they'd get. He heard the rest of the men stomping through the woods behind him.

Preacher was stunned when he reached the hidden trap door. Dragon pulled it open and motioned him in. He was horrified as he descended into the cold, dark basement. He couldn't believe his girl and Snake had spent three days down here.

The first room Preacher was shown was where Pike had kept Snake. The chains still hung from the ceiling, and there was blood on the floor. He silently left that room and followed Dragon to another room.

As he entered, he knew this was where Macy had been kept. It was damp, dirty and dark. Preacher saw red. There was a cot, and nothing else.

"You like what you see?" Steele taunted, causing Preacher to turn to his VP furiously.

"You fucking know I don't?" he snarled.

"Good," Steele grunted. "Come on." Then he was led back outside.

Preacher froze when they cleared the basement and Dagger was standing there with the fucking rocket launcher.

"Hey prez," Dagger cheerfully greeted. "Heard you're moping around. That's not helping your girl at all. Sitting around all sad and quiet isn't fucking like you. You're the god damned president of the baddest motorcycle club around, fucking act like it."

Preacher glared at Dagger furiously as he balled his fists.

"Get fucking pissed," Dagger continued. "Your girl was down there for three days. Pike tried to rape her, and now she's fighting for her life. Use that anger and take this," Dagger ordered as he handed him the rocket launcher. "Start by blowing up that fucking hell hole."

Preacher smirked as he looked at all his brothers. They were right, he knew it, and it was time to let his anger take over. He snatched the rocket launcher out of Dagger's hands, aimed at the bunker, and fired.

The explosion was fucking awesome. The bunker disappeared in a cloud of black smoke, along with half the surrounding trees, and a ball of fire rose high into the air. When the smoke finally cleared, both the trees and bunker were gone. It was the best thing Preacher had ever witnessed.

"You better now?" Dagger questioned as he shot a smile his way.

"Hell yes," Preacher growled.

"Good, now go back to that fucking hospital and wake your girl up," Steele ordered. "She's been asleep fucking long enough."

Preacher grinned at his brothers, feeling better for the first time in days.

"Fucking bikers," he chuckled. "Smartest fuckers in the world."

Then he turned and strode back to his Harley. It was time to take their advice.

Chapter Fifty
Preacher

Preacher stepped off the elevator and was headed down the hall when his phone rang. He pulled it out, glanced at the screen, and saw it was Darren. Sighing, he answered it.

"I don't have time for this," Preacher growled in annoyance.

"Yeah, well do you have time to explain the ball of fire that shot out of woods where near Macy was found?" the detective questioned.

"Dagger gave me a rocket launcher. I used it," Preacher answered simply. He chuckled when there was silence on the other end of the phone, then Colin started cursing. "Got me on speaker?" he eventually asked, knowing that's what Darren had done.

"Jesus," Darren complained, "not anymore." Then he yelled, obviously to Colin. "Shut up or get the fuck out of here."

"Right," Darren stated addressing Preacher again. "So some kids were messing around with one of the old distilleries and it blew."

"Works for me," Preacher grinned, before promptly hanging up.

"Darren came up with something?" Steele asked as he caught up to him.

"Fuckers got a good imagination," Preacher returned. "Need you to get a crew and get moving on the fucking attic renovations," he ordered. "Navaho's good, I want him in charge."

"Done," Steele told him. "You ready for this?"

"Absolutely," Preacher smirked as he pushed open the door and prowled into his girls room. He wasn't surprised to see her still asleep. He nodded at Snake when the brother lifted his head.

Preacher headed straight to the bed and looked down at his Hummingbird. Nothing had changed, and that pissed him off more. The brothers had riled him up, and he was ready to do battle. He leaned down and got close to her ear.

"Fucking wake up Hummingbird," he roared. "I'm fucking sick and tired of watching you lie there. I've waited my whole life for you, and you're not fucking dying on me."

Snake pushed out of his chair furiously and headed straight for him, but Steele and Dragon caught him and slammed him roughly against the wall.

"You wake up right the fuck now, or I'm walking out the god damned door," Preacher continued. "I'm not fucking sitting here watching you die. You know what that will do to me."

"Mother fucker," Snake roared. "I'm going to fucking gut you."

Snake was livid now and was cursing up a storm as he threatened Preacher's life and struggled against Steele and Dragon. The brothers weren't going to be able to hold him much longer.

Suddenly the machines hooked up to his Hummingbird started going nuts. Preacher stared at his girl and willed her to wake. A finger twitched, and that's all he needed. He climbed on the bed and positioned his body over hers. He covered her completely, so all she could feel was him.

"Come on Hummingbird," Preacher coaxed. "You want me to stay, you wake the fuck up and tell me. Open those eyes so I can see you," he ordered.

Macy's eyelids fluttered for a minute, and then slowly opened. Preacher's heart literally stopped as she glared up at him.

"You leave and I'm going to call you an ass from now on," she hoarsely whispered. Then she promptly broke into tears.

Preacher rolled onto his side and wrapped his arms gently around her. Then he buried his face in her long hair.

"Jesus christ Hummingbird," he growled. "You scared the ever living shit out of me."

"Don't leave," she sobbed in return.

"Wasn't planning on it," Preacher smirked. "Right by your side is where I'll always be."

Then he was knocked off the bed as Snake dove at him. The brother punched him in the jaw before he could even react. All hell broke loose, as Dragon and

Steele tried to pull Snake off, and all the other brothers waiting in the hall came charging in.

It took the staff fifteen minutes to sort things out and clear the room. When Preacher finally made it back to his Hummingbird, he had several more bruises to add to the collection.

"My brothers turning into a bruiser," his girl whispered, as she patted the bed beside her.

"Your brothers turning into something," Preacher growled as he climbed back on the bed. It was then he noticed her eyes were getting heavy again.

"I love you bossy pants," she sighed.

When he raised a brow in question, she only smiled. "I'm tired and I can't think of anything good."

Preacher pulled her close against his chest and got comfortable. "Sleep Hummingbird," he ordered. "I'll be right here when you wake up."

Chapter Fifty One
Macy

Macy was absolutely sick of the hospital. It had been two days, and she was ready to leave this place. Of course having Preacher stay with her had helped. Doc had tried to bring in a spare bed for him, but he had refused, and Doc said he wasn't surprised. She was still extremely tired, but the infection in her back was almost gone.

Macy turned to the door as Doc suddenly walked in. Preacher looked up too from his perch on the end of her bed.

"How are you feeling Sweetheart?" Doc gently asked.

"Good," Macy replied, then sighed when Preacher growled from the end of the bed. "Tired, and extremely weak," she reluctantly admitted.

"That's to be expected," Doc informed her. "Your body seems to shut down when it gets sick. How about we get you out of here and get you back to the compound? You're out of danger, and I can keep an eye on you just as easily there."

Macy grinned at him, then looked to Preacher.

"Sounds perfect," Preacher agreed with a smile of his own.

"Sounds perfect," she repeated to Doc. He chuckled and looked at Preacher.

"I need to stay a bit longer, but I'll send you home with some meds and check on when I get there. You want to drive my SUV back?" he asked.

"Yep," Preacher confirmed as he dug his keys out of his pocket and threw them over. "Be careful with my Harley."

Doc grinned. "I'm a little too old to be doing wheelies," he chuckled.

"We can't take the bike?" Macy asked sadly.

"Hummingbird, you can barely hold your head up without falling asleep. I refuse to let you on the back until your better," Preacher told her.

"Okay," she easily agreed. "But you're going to have a hard time keeping me off when I am."

"That's not a hardship," Preacher growled.

The next little while consisted of Preacher signing her out and helping her get dressed. Then he carried her down to the car. Of course there was a nurse chasing them with a wheelchair and yelling about protocol, but Preacher just ignored her.

As soon as they pulled out of the lot, they were surrounded by most of the club. It surprised Macy that so many bikers were there. When her brother pulled up next to her door and stayed there, she grinned and blew him a kiss. Of course Preacher yelled at her, but she didn't care. She had her brother back, and she wanted him to know how happy she was.

When they arrived Preacher carried her in, and all the brothers clapped and cheered. He headed straight to his room, which she was extremely happy about. Unfortunately, she was ready for a nap already. Preacher pushed open the door, and once more peered around it before entering.

"Why do you keep doing that?" Macy sighed.

"Because of this," he growled as he pushed the door open fully and stepped inside.

Her jaw dropped as she looked around. The walls were painted a soft purple. There was a purple comforter and tons of pillows on the bed. A beautiful chandelier hung from the ceiling that was a mixture of glass prisms and purple crystals. But the best part was the dozens of teddy bears. They all wore purple shirts, and everyone of them had a different thing written on it.

"Does that say Snuggle Bunny?" Macy asked in surprise. Then she read another. "Hot Lips, Lady Killer, Sexy Thing, Baby Cakes, Kissy Face. Oh my god," she cried. "I've got so many new names to call you."

"We're helpful like that," Dagger yelled from the hall. Then all the bikers that had snuck down to watch snorted.

"Jesus Christ," Preacher loudly cursed. "Fucking bikers."

"I love it," Macy squealed as he gently laid her on the bed. She watched as the sun hit the chandelier, and it made little rainbows all over the walls. "Can we take all this upstairs and use it in the loft when it's finished."

"We'll help you pack it up," Dagger yelled, and she knew Preacher was about to lose his patience.

As Macy watched, he walked to the door and slammed it in all their faces. Then he came back to settle on the bed beside her.

"You really love it, don't you?" he asked with a small frown.

"I really do," she admitted.

"They always do," Preacher huffed. Then he proceeded to tell her the story of all the other rooms and how this all started. Apparently, nobody could figure out who was doing it though.

Chapter Fifty Two
Preacher

Preacher was extremely worried about his Hummingbird's health. She was tired and weak. Doc assured him it was normal, and she would remain this way for a while. When she was better, Doc explained he could get her on some vitamins. They would help build up her immune system and help her battle colds better.

She was asleep again, and he was grateful. He'd been itching since he found her to get his hands on Pike, and it looked like today was the day. He left his sister with her and wandered out to the common room. All heads lifted as soon as he stepped inside.

"Time to play?" Steele questioned as he came up beside him.

"Been fucking looking forward to this," Preacher grinned.

He took off his vest, folded it, and stashed it behind the bar. When he headed outside, Steele was right beside him.

"Doc gave him some antibiotics. Fucker was starting to get an infection in his eye. He may not have lasted if Doc hadn't," Steele explained.

Preacher nodded. "Right."

Dragon came up on his other side. "Snake's already inside."

Preacher pushed open the door and stepped into the shed. He looked at Pike hanging from the chains, then froze. He'd heard enough about the spring his girl had shoved into the man's eye, but seeing it in person was something else entirely. He stepped up to Pike and wiggled the spring a little. The fucker screamed so loud Preacher was ready to cover his ears.

"Wanted to see if it was as painful as it looked," Preacher chuckled. "Apparently it is."

He was so proud of Hummingbird. The spring was actually pushed right into his eyeball. The socket was red, and the entire area around it was inflamed.

"My Hummingbird was as meant for me," Preacher proudly declared. Then he noticed Snake in the corner. "You want a part of him first? You can have some time, but he's mine to end," Preacher told Macy's brother.

"Nope," Snake easily replied. "I got revenge when I was younger, and I still took him down chained like he is now. I'm good," he assured him. "But I'm definitely staying to watch."

Preacher nodded and turned back to Pike. "You thought you could take something that belonged to me?" he demanded. He grinned when Pike only glared. "My girl hasn't lived a good life, but she has me now, and that's going to fucking change," Preacher growled.

He then raised his hand and gave the spring a little flick, once more Pike screamed in pain. Preacher couldn't help laughing. Afterwards, he moved in front of him and rained blow after blow into the fuckers stomach. He smirked when he heard Pike's ribs crack.

"I'm old school," Preacher explained to Pike. "I don't like the blowtorch like Dragon here does." Dragon just shrugged like he didn't have a care in the world. "Steele here likes blades. Me, I prefer a hammer," Preacher explained as he moved to the work bench and picked one up.

Preacher wasn't in the mood to fuck around. He leaned down and smashed every toe on the fuckers feet. Navaho had to throw water at Pike twice when he lost consciousness.

Preacher grinned up at Pike as he took a break. "How you doing there fucker?" he taunted. "You regret messing with my girl now?"

Pike was sputtering and mumbling and Preacher couldn't understand a word the fucker was saying, so he gave the spring another flick. Pike jerked in the chains and screamed once more.

"I'm fucking sorry. Just let me go," Pike pleaded. "I won't go anywhere near her again."

Preacher threw back his head and laughed. "You think I'm letting you go," he questioned. Then his expression turned murderous. "You're fucking dying here today."

Preacher turned to the bench, picked up a screwdriver, and drove it into the fuckers right knee. Snake helpfully passed him another one, and he did the same to the other knee. Then he reached up and pulled the spring out of his eye. The eye came with it, along with the membrane and a shit ton of blood.

"Jesus," Snake growled. "That's fucking disgusting."

Preacher pulled the gun he always kept in the waistband of his jeans out and looked at Pike one more time. The fucker was loosing consciousness again, and Preacher knew the man didn't have much longer. He shoved the barrel into the bloody cavity where his eye had once been and pulled the trigger.

"I like old school," Snake declared happily. "That was fucking awesome."

Preacher stared at the brother awhile, then he threw back his head and laughed.

Chapter Fifty Three
Macy

Macy woke slowly and groaned. She was achy and tired, but she knew from experience that's what happened after being hospitalized. She looked to the corner of the room when she realized someone was sitting there.

"Dad," she exclaimed in surprise. "I thought you were still in the hospital?"

"I checked myself out," he shrugged.

"Are you well enough to be out?" Macy questioned as she eyed him critically. He looked pale, and she knew he had to be in pain.

"Probably not," her dad honestly admitted. "I'm hiding from Doc."

"Well, this wouldn't be the best place to hide," Macy advised him. "Doc pops in to check on me all the time."

He nodded in understanding. "I'll get right down to it then. I'm so sorry this happened to you. A father is supposed to protect his children, not put their lives in danger."

Macy instantly frowned. "That's not what happened."

"It is," he argued. "It was my gambling debt that got you into trouble. Pike wanted his money back, and because I couldn't pay, he took you."

"But that was his doing, not yours. He's the one to change the rules. You said no and tried to pay him back. When he wouldn't accept it you came here and warned me, even though you were hurt," Macy argued.

"That's true," her dad agreed. "But my gambling started it all, and that's on me."

"So why are you telling me this?" she asked anxiously.

"I'm leaving," he outright told her.

Macy struggled to sit up and was thankful when her dad moved to help her. She leaned up against the mound of pillows Preacher had piled near the headboard. Her back was better, and the infection was gone, but it was still tender.

"You can't go," Macy immediately told him, then watched as he gave her a sad smile.

"I'm going to try to be a better father," he declared. "And that means getting myself some help."

"What do you mean?" she curiously asked.

"I'm going to a rehab facility about a couple hours from here. I've already called and made all the arrangements. They're expecting me later today," he explained.

Macy instantly felt tears run down her cheeks. "Will I see you again?"

Her dad moved close immediately and gently pulled her into his arms. She clung to him as he kissed her head.

"I'll be in lockdown for six months," he explained. "That means absolutely no contact with family and friends. I'll need to put everything I have into the program and concentrate solely on it. They tell me family equals distractions."

"So I can't call or see you?" she asked, not liking that at all.

"I'm doing this for you honey," he soothed. "Once the time is up, they allow calls. A couple weeks after that I can have visitors."

Something else occurred to her, and she pushed back so there was some distance between them.

"How are you paying for this?" she questioned. "A program like that sounds expensive."

"I can't tell you," he grinned. "It's a secret."

Macy narrowed her eyes at him. "Did you steal the money?" she demanded.

He immediately lost his grin. "No," he told her.

"Well Snake doesn't have that kind of money," she pushed.

"He doesn't," her dad agreed.

Macy stared at him a minute, as she tried to figure it out. Suddenly it hit her. There was only one other man who would do this to make her happy.

"Preacher's paying for it," she huffed, knowing in her heart it was him.

"It's a secret," he told her again.

Macy shook her head as her dad grinned at her.

"I've got to go," her dad told her as he looked her over one more time. "The bikers fixed my car and I've got my bag in it already," explained.

She pulled him close again, and he held her tight against his chest. When he pulled back, she knew he was done with goodbyes.

"I love you honey. You stick with your brother and that biker of yours, and you'll be just fine," he promised.

"You trust him," Macy questioned in surprise.

"He took a bullet to the head for you," her dad grinned. Then he stood and headed to the door.

"I love you too dad," she whispered.

He turned back, winked, and then walked out the door.

Chapter Fifty Four
Preacher

Preacher showered out behind the shed, then headed to the common room. His Hummingbird should be awake by now, and he was anxious to see how she was doing. He wanted to get her outside for a bit of fresh air, and he wanted to check in with Navaho on how the second floor renovations were coming along. As soon as Pike was grabbed, a lot of brothers found themselves with more free time, and had pitched in to help.

Just before Preacher reached the door, Steele headed in his direction. He slowed and waited for his VP, annoyed that he was being delayed from reaching his girl.

"You good?" Steele questioned, as he pounded him on the shoulder.

"I am," Preacher admitted. His bruises were finally fading, his ribs didn't ache as much, and the stitches came out of his head just that morning.

"Have to warn you, Darren and Colin are inside," Steele warmed.

"What the fuck do they want?" Preacher sighed.

"Didn't ask," Steele admitted with a shrug.

Preacher pushed inside and headed to the table they were sitting at. He wasn't surprised to see Wrench, Lucifer and Klutz sitting with them. Wrench and his sister were laughing, but of course Lucifer was silently glaring at Colin. That brother still considered Colin a threat, even though he had married his girl. Darren saw him first and nodded to him as he joined them.

"Hear Pike got caught up in that still explosion that happened a couple days ago. Fire burned so hot there's nothing left. The only thing we found was his vehicle, that was parked not far away. His finger prints were all over it."

"That's a shame," Preacher grinned. "So that's all you're here for?"

"No," Colin answered. "We actually want to talk to Snake a bit about Pike's operation. With Pike dead, we're hoping we can easily round up his men and completely shut everything down."

"Well I'm all for that," Preacher announced. "I'll send Snake over. He's out of the hospital and usually hangs in the garage."

"How's your girl?" Darren asked in concern.

"Tired and weak," Preacher admitted. "Apparently, when she gets a cold, it escalates quickly. Takes her body a long time to recover."

"There going to be another wedding soon?" Lucifer asked.

"Hell yes," Preacher smirked. "But she needs to be feeling better for that."

Darren and Colin stood, and it was obvious they were headed to the garage to track down Snake. Preacher stood too and moved towards the hall, of course he could hear Lucifer from the other side of the room.

"You don't need to say goodbye to her," Lucifer yelled.

"I've known her forever, and she's my friend," Colin complained.

Preacher moved out of hearing distance, not wanting to be around when fists started flying. Every time those two got close to each other a fight broke out.

When Preacher opened the door to his room, he found his Hummingbird propped up on the pillows. He looked at her then frowned, hurrying over to the bed and sitting down.

"You've been crying," he growled as he carefully pulled her close. Of course those were the wrong words to say, because immediately she started crying again.

"You're paying for my dad to go to rehab," she whispered once she had calmed down. He pushed her hair off her face and kissed her forehead.

"Wes isn't a bad guy," Preacher admitted. "He just has a problem. Figure if he can get that solved he'll be the kind of dad you and your brother deserve."

"Can you afford that?" Macy asked. "The way he described it I'm sure it's expensive."

"I'm paying part of it and Cassie's paying the rest. She has a lot of money. She wanted to use it to help out some of the brothers with their cabins, but the cabins are small and don't cost a lot. Most of the brothers can afford it," Preacher explained.

"How will I thank her?" Macy asked in complete shock. "That's extremely generous of her." Preacher watched as she seemed to get an idea and brighten.

"Marry me good looking," she cried. "She can be my bride's maid."

"First of all, I ask you, not the other way around. And second of all, you're going to piss off my sister by asking Cassie."

"Shoot," Macy huffed causing Preacher to chuckle.

Then he reached in his pocket and pulled out the ring he had made for her. It had a diamond in the middle, and the sides contained two small hummingbirds.

"Marry me," Preacher ordered. Then he was knocked back as she launched herself at him.

"Yes, baby cakes," she cried as more tears flowed. But Preacher didn't care, his girl would finally be his.

Chapter Fifty Five
Macy

It was a week later, and Macy was feeling better. She was still tired, but she could move around more. Preacher took her outside every day, and she loved the fresh air. She even got to ride in the scoop of a tractor they had at the compound. She just had to wait for them to remove the chunks of drywall from it. They laid blankets inside, and she was quite comfortable as they toured the compound. From what Dragon told her, they had done the same thing for Ali because her leg was bad.

Dinner had just been finished, and the brothers were hanging out and having some drinks. Macy was sitting with the girls, and they were giggling as she told them all about Preacher's room. The girls were in hysterics as she told them about the chandelier, and how it made pretty rainbow patterns around the

room. November immediately decided she was
getting Jude to buy one for them.

Suddenly Preacher was at the front of the room
calling for attention. Steele was standing right beside
him.

"Smoke," he bellowed. "Get your ass up here."
Smoke looked up in surprise, then made his way to
the front of the room.

"You've been an asset to this club since you joined it,
and I'm fucking glad you chose to go with us, instead
of being a suit wearing monkey for Mario," Preacher
smirked.

"Fuck off," Mario yelled from a corner of the room.
Alex was at their table and she laughed. As soon as
she did, his head swivelled her way, and he winked at
her.

"We understand you had to leave to take care of
your grandmother, and we told you that wouldn't
fuck up your probation. Well the years up and
you've done everything we asked of you. We'd be
fucking proud if you'd accept a new vest and become
a fully patched brother," Preacher declared.

Smoke looked overwhelmed, but he finally scrambled
to take off his prospect vest, and drop it on the table

closest to him. Steele opened a box and handed Preacher a new one. Preacher then helped Smoke into it, as the biker grinned proudly.

"Welcome to the Knight's," Preacher roared.

Immediately Smoke disappeared from view, as the bikers shouted congratulations and surrounded him. Preacher allowed this for a few minutes and then called for silence again.

"Hummingbird?" Preacher bellowed at her once things quieted. "Get your pretty little ass up here."

Macy turned beet red as she looked towards Preacher. She wasn't used to the attention, and it was a bit unnerving. She squealed when someone pulled her chair back. She looked up to find Snake there.

"Come on sis," he grunted as he held his hand out to her. "I'll go up with you." She smiled at him gratefully and placed her hand in his.

When they reached the front, Steele moved to the side and Snake took his place. She slowly moved to stand with Preacher.

"You're going to marry me next week Hummingbird, and that means you'll be a full member. As my girl, you'll be the queen of the club, and it's fucking time you had a vest so everyone knows you belong to me," he growled.

Macy blinked up at him. "But I already took care of that," she said.

She pulled down the neck of her shirt so it exposed the back of her shoulder. There she had a new tattoo with Preacher's name, and a small hummingbird underneath it. He peered at the tattoo, then looked at her in astonishment.

"When the fuck did you do that?" he questioned.

"You guys were busy this morning," she told him. "All us girls got one."

Suddenly chaos ensued as chairs were pushed back, and bikers made their way to their women. Each girl had tattooed their bikers name, along with a symbol for the name their biker nicknamed them.

Macy tilted her head and blinked up at him. "Was it okay we did that?" she asked nervously.

Preacher growled and pulled her close. "You were fucking made to be mine," he said as he slammed his lips down on hers.

Then Macy squealed when he picked her up and headed for their room. It surprised her when she noticed the rest of the bikers dragging their women out as well.

"I'll just hold on to the vest until you come back," her brother bellowed after them. Macy waved her hand in thanks as they disappeared down the hall.

Epilogue

Exactly one week later, Preacher and Macy were married. With Preacher being the groom, he couldn't officiate the ceremony, so they had to figure that part out. Luckily Doc stepped forward. Apparently he had gotten his licence when he started working at the hospital. Some patients wanted to be given their last rights, and some wanted to get married. It helped if they had a minister on hand.

Preacher stood outside on the grass by the lake. The twinkling lights had been set up, and the trees were once more adorned in paper lanterns. When it was time for Macy to walk out, she came around the corner on her brother's arm. Preacher stated at her momentarily, then he busted out laughing. His girl was definitely made for him.

She wore her hair down, and it blew slightly in the breeze, but it was the jeans, biker boots, vest and tight club tank top that got his attention. She turned slightly, and he got a clear view of the beautiful tattoo she had gotten for him.

As soon as his girl got close, he yanked her out of Snake's hold and slammed his lips down on hers. She immediately melted against him and returned the kiss with the same enthusiasm. When he pulled back, she smiled up at him.

"Fucking perfect," he growled. She blinked and tilted her head, and he was forced to kiss her again.

"This is going to take all night," Dagger complained. "You do that after the vows," he grumbled as he threw up his hands. Several brothers chuckled, but Preacher ignored them.

Preacher eventually turned back to Doc, and the ceremony continued. It was short, but it was fucking perfect. As soon as it was over he kissed her once more, then scooped her up and headed for the loft. She hadn't seen it yet, but the brothers and him had worked hard to get it done in time.

He climbed the outside stairs and set her down on the new deck. It was huge, and it ran the entire width of the clubhouse. They watched for a few minutes as the men moved the chairs and got ready for the bonfire.

"It's such a perfect view," Macy sighed in contentment.

"It certainly is," Preacher agreed as he stared at her. He smirked when she ducked her head and blushed. "Come see inside," he ordered as he held out her hand.

"What's that?" she asked, as she pointed to something by the sliding doors. He grinned and pulled her over to them.

"These are hummingbird feeders," Preacher explained as he pointed them out. He had three mounted on the outside wall. "I want you to be able to see them from inside the house too." He smiled as tears formed in her eyes.

"That's amazing," she whispered.

Inside he showed her the kitchen, that had the farmhouse sink she asked for. The cupboards were made of light pine in order to keep the space brighter, and the counter was a large butcher block. It ran down one whole side of the loft. The entire area was open, and the living room sat on the opposite side. The loft was wide enough that there was a ton of space for both.

The living room had a fireplace, two large comfy leather sofas, a skylight, and the chandelier was hanging in the centre. Preacher had checked it carefully to make sure it was in a position to catch the right light. Of course she wouldn't know that until the morning. There was a bathroom at the back, along with a master bedroom and two smaller bedrooms. The master had a small bathroom attached as well.

Preacher knew she was in awe of the bedroom, because she stepped inside then stopped. Navaho had helped him build a beautiful wood frame for the bed. Preacher had wanted it to be special, so he had asked Navaho to carve a hummingbird into the headboard. The brother was fucking talented, and it had turned out beautifully. A large skylight had been placed in the room too, and they could see the stars from the bed.

"This is the special project you were working on when we got tattooed?" she asked.

"It is," he told her.

Macy ran at him then and tackled him to the bed. "I love you Snookums."

Preacher chuckled at the name. "I love you too Hummingbird." And then he proceeded to show her just how much.

Three weeks later they found out they'd made a baby that night.

About the Author

MEGAN FALL is a mother of three who helps her husband run his construction business. She has been writing all her life, but with a push from her daughter, started publishing. It's the best thing she ever did. When she's not writing, you can find her at the beach. She loves searching for rocks, sea glass, driftwood and fossils. She believes in ghosts, collects ridiculous amounts of plants, and rides on the back of her hubby's motorcycle.

MEGAN FALL

Look for these books coming soon!

STONE KNIGHTS MC SERIES
Finding Ali
Saving Cassie
Loving Misty
Rescuing Tiffany
Guarding Alexandria
Protecting Fable
Surviving November
Sheltering Macy
Defending Zoe
Treasuring Maggie

DEVILS SOLDIERS MC SERIES
Resisting Diesel
Surviving Hawk

THE ENFORCER SERIES
The Enforcer
The Enforcers Revenge

Defending Zoe
Stone Knight's Book 9

Chapter One
Dagger

Dagger snarled as he found himself locked in his room again. He sat on the floor and breathed in the quiet for a few minutes. The club was expanding a lot, and most of his brothers now had their own women. Things were changing, and he knew it was for the better, he just didn't know if he would ever find the same thing.

Only a handful of brothers knew he was a marine. He liked to keep that part of his life private. He had been stationed in Afghanistan with his best friend Ty. They grew up together and were thick as thieves. When Ty became a marine, Dagger followed. A month before they were finished their tour, the vehicle they were in got taken out by a roadside bomb. Dagger hadn't even gotten a scratch, but Ty had died.

Dagger had been lost for a long time, suffering, and not knowing where to turn. Then one day Preacher walked into his life and basically saved him. He had found a home with The Stone Knight's, and had healed. He learned to laugh again and had gained a ton of new brothers.

Now he was known as the comedian of the club. He went out of his way to make sure he kept things light. He could forget when things were crazy, and the brothers were laughing. It helped keep him sane.

But when it was quiet, like it was now, Dagger savoured it. Sometimes he wanted to just breathe and remember Ty. He always complained when they pulled this shit, but secretly he sometimes needed it.

Figuring he had been in the room long enough he climbed to his feet and walked into the bathroom. He grabbed the nearest towel, wrapped it around his arm, and walked over to the bedroom window. Without much effort, he pulled back and slammed his elbow into the glass. It shattered immediately, and he efficiently pulled the leftover shards out of the way. When the frame was clean, he dropped the towel over the sill and climbed out.

In minutes he was walking in the main doors. Dragon noticed him first, and his head spun from him to the back hall, and to him again.

"I thought you were in your room?" Dragon frowned. "Where the hell did you come from?"

Dagger just grinned. "I have dynamite you idiots. You know you can't hold me down for long." He sat at the bar and motioned for Smoke to grab him a shot of whiskey.

"If you blew a hole through the goddamned wall, I'm going to rip you a new asshole," Preacher growled as he sat down beside him.

Dagger smirked at his president. "I'd never do that," he lied in mock horror. "Besides, I have a date with a hottie. I can't break her heart by not showing up."

"Who's it this time?" Dragon questioned. "The clerk at the convenience store, the bartender, or one of the dancers at the strip club?"

"They had their chance," Dagger smirked with a wave of his hand. "This is a new girl I've been seeing for about a month now."

"You going to bring her around so we can meet her?" Trike asked as he joined them.

"Nah," Dagger denied. "It's just a girl I'm having some fun with."

"You'll find the right one soon," Trike smirked. "And I bet she's going be a handful.

"Right," Steele added. "I want to see you with someone who gives you a run for your money."

Dagger chuckled. "Not likely," he told them. "My girls going to be sweet, soft, and quiet." All the bikers within hearing distance snorted.

"Your girls going to be a hell raiser," Sniper snickered. "I bet you one hundred dollars she's worse than you," he said, as he slapped a hundred dollar bill on the bar. Immediately six more hundreds landed on top of the first one.

"You fuckers suck," Dagger complained. "I'll take that bet, and you all can kiss my ass when I prove you wrong."

"You're going to have to sell your Harley to come up with the money you will owe us all," Steele teased.

"Fucking bikers," Dagger growled as he pushed off his stool and made his way to the door. As he opened it he heard the bikers laughter following him.

It wouldn't happen, he thought to himself. His sweet girl was out there, and he'd fucking find her.